M.C

My Wife's Desires

Book 3

First published by Steffy Ink Publishing LLC 2021

This novel is entirely a work of fiction. The names, characters and incidents portrayed in it are the work of the author's imagination. Any resemblance to actual persons, living or dead, events or localities is entirely coincidental.

M.C. Rivera asserts the moral right to be identified as the author of this work.

First edition

*This book was professionally typeset on Reedsy.
Find out more at reedsy.com*

"In all the world, there is no heart for me like yours. In all the world, there is no love for you like mine." – Maya Angelou

One

Nick: Poly-Troubles

⁂

I stand behind the bar, watching Katie instruct two of my employees. They raise the banner, tying it off, a centerpiece to the decorations surrounding it. 'Congratulations, Tyler!'

Her smile is contagious, and all attention follows her. She glows like usual. She should have been a motivational speaker, a CEO at some company, or a nurse out there saving lives, but instead, she's a housewife with empty nest syndrome.

How could I deny her anything?

"Hey, boss, it's almost time. You wanted to change?"

"Yeah, thanks, Marco."

I quickly end inventory, leaving my bartender to finish setting up. My clothes for tonight hang up on the wall in my office. Just as I'm about to shut the door, Katie walks in. "I think we're done. What time is he supposed to be here?"

She knows the answer, but in her effort to keep me involved, she asks.

And in an effort to stay out of it, I shrug, "Don't know."

I peel off my dirty shirt and reach for my button-up, but Katie's hands are on my back, slipping around my chest and hugging me. Her supple breasts press into me as she whispers in my ear, "Thank you for doing this."

"He deserves it. Not everybody can make it through medical school."

"That's not what I'm talking about." She rotates me, and I glance at the clock. I got to open in five minutes. She directs my eyes back to hers, "Not everybody would allow their wife a second husband." She grins, kissing me, lingering. Her brown eyes admire my face. I love it when she looks at me like this. "You are my Soulmate. You know that? You understand me the way no one else does."

"I'm a god among men."

Katie giggles, falling into me. "The only thing I wish for is you to open up more. Sometimes I don't know what you're thinking, and it scares me. Promise me that you're happy."

"Of course, I'm happy."

She runs her hand down to my dick, gripping the flaccid snake, "You better be."

I grab her boob in response. "What I'm thinking about right now is I'm running out of time."

She snaps her head to the clock, "I got to get all the guests into their places!" She rushes out.

Katie wants me to talk.

Tyler wants me to talk.

But I don't want to talk.

After I dress, I sit in my chair, and the final minute I have, I pray.

2

Hanging on to God has been the only thing keeping me afloat. It's blasphemy, I know. I'm committing sin after sin and then praying God will forgive me. What I'm doing with Katie and Tyler is perhaps the most offensive thing I can do against God besides killing someone. Yet, I can't seem to stop it. I keep getting deeper. I'm sinking in quicksand and making no attempt to save myself.

How can I admit that I'm happy with our arrangement? What normal person would allow another man to fuck his wife? That, in and of itself, is a sin. But for some awful reason, I enjoy it. Watching Katie and Tyler fuck has become a fetish, an addiction, and I don't want to stop.

Another sin on top of many is how I feel about Tyler. Words I don't like to think about: attraction, love, desire. Gay ass words that shouldn't correlate to another man. But for some reason, they do.

How am I supposed to say it out loud? I know I shouldn't be this way. But denying it, turning it away, isn't what I want to do.

It would be easier without faith. I could look at myself in the mirror without shame.

But I was raised to do right by God, so how can I live the way I want and still be faithful?

My father is helping me readjust. He has been praying and reading the bible. It's a valiant effort to understand me and the things that I'm going through. Because of him that I'm accepting the direction my life is heading. He believes that part of our reason for meeting Tyler is to help him succeed at becoming a doctor. He sees what we are doing as a good deed. Only my dad would find some divine interruption out of our threesome.

3

A quick knock on the door gets me to my feet.

Tyler arrives and acts completely surprised by the celebration, even though I ruined it by mentioning it. I hadn't known it was supposed to be a secret. Katie got all pissy with me, but thankfully, his reaction makes up for it, and she is beaming with admiration.

Marco stands beside me in the back and grunts, "I'd turn gay for that too."

I roll my eyes, "You say that every time he walks in the restaurant. First off, I'm not gay, and second, do you say that when I walk in?"

"Why do you think I still work here?" He winks.

I shove him, "When do you work? Lazy ass."

Katie finds me across the restaurant and waves to me, but I shake my head. I'm working despite this being a celebration. She clings to Tyler's arm as he thanks each person individually. We got a few of his classmates to attend, a few old friends, his brother and his family, and some of our family members to show up.

Katie once more waves to me, a bit more adamant this time, and without an excuse, I grab a bottle of wine and three glasses and head over.

Tyler is talking to his brother. Katie helps me by grabbing the glasses, and I open the wine bottle. The pop spooks him, and he turns to me. "Hey, man," he hugs me, kissing my cheek, "This place looks great."

"All Katie." I pour us all a glass and lift it, "To Tyler. Let's pray he doesn't kill anybody."

He hangs his head laughing. Before he takes a sip, he turns to the crowd, "Thank you, everybody, for coming. It's taking me a long time, but I made it. And I have only two people to thank for that. Nick and Katie. Mentally I would have failed. Financially, I would have failed."

I laugh, nodding—the most expensive escort in history.

"Emotionally, I would have failed. These two people took me in when I had nothing and gave me everything. I can't wait to marry them if only to prove I haven't been using them."

The chuckles are awkward and weak. It's how I feel most of the time. I know Tyler loves to talk about our arrangement, but no one, and I mean no one, is as open and excited as he is. Well, except Marco, our only gay server, who at the moment hoops and hollers in the back and then adds, "I better be invited to the wedding."

"Thank you," Tyler takes a drink, and we all follow. He leans in and kisses Katie, whispering 'Thank you' against her lips. Then he steps to me and kisses me as well. After that, I back out, avoiding everyones' eyes, and make an excuse to go back to work.

For the most part, I don't care what people think. It's what I think that bothers me. We are two men, and we shouldn't be kissing. But the more it happens, the less I mind. The more he pushes, the less I push back. It's easier. I don't feel as much guilt if I put it all on his shoulders.

For the most part, the party stays in the private room in the back, but as more people show up, it trickles out into the main dining room, bothering some of my customers. I keep up with their happiness, taking fifty percent off their bill. In a place like this, where checks usually range between a hundred and fifty to three hundred, half-off makes them feel much better.

Katie is on her way to the bathroom when she passes by me and whispers in song, "Tyler's getting drunk."

Tyler hasn't been drunk in a long time; even the night we

went to the club, he stayed relatively sober, so I'm happy he's feeling relaxed enough to drink. However, he gets flirty and loses filters. It's best to stay away so he doesn't embarrass me.

I sit in my office, and as soon as Katie leaves the bathroom, I call her over. "Maybe you should take him home."

"It's still early. He's having fun. Besides, my sister wants me to go pick her up. She wants to drink and sleep over tonight."

"You can't leave."

"Tyler's a big boy. He can take care of himself." She comes up and kisses me. "His brother and David are here. I'll ask them to keep watch." Her hands slip down my chest, moving for my cock, "You afraid he'll get all handsy?"

I'm cackling as I move out of her hands, "Yes, that's exactly what I'm worried about. Are you sure you can drive?"

"I haven't had a drink in weeks. Never know when something's baking in the oven. Bye!"

I stare after her. I hate that there is something in this world that I can't give her. It's why at times, I am thankful for Tyler. There are times where I think, or perhaps hope that God sent him to us to give us a baby. Those are the times when I can show Tyler that I do feel something.

The night continues, and Tyler gets drunker. Even from across the restaurant, I can hear him. He loves to tell his escort stories to eager crowds, the ones that are the craziest and, more than likely, the most disgusting. If we weren't at my restaurant, I would be laughing along with the rest of them, but here is not the place. The customers closest to the room are the most disturbed, and I am quick to tell my floor manager to find them another spot. We are at full capacity, but I can shift some tables, perhaps even put tables outside.

When Tyler heads to the bathroom, I follow behind and wait

for him in my office. The moment he comes out, I wave him over and shut the door behind me. "Hey, I need you to—"

He's kissing me aggressively, "Where have you been?" Tyler pants into my lips, "I'm so fucking horny," he snatches my hand, placing it on his hardon, "Grip it. Come on, Nick," his lips are all over my throat.

I squeeze, if only to make him hiss. "You gotta stop with your stories. You're upsetting some guests."

"Sure," He moans, clearly not listening. "Where's Katie? I wanted to bury my cock in her in the bathroom."

"No fucking in my restaurant."

"You sure?" Tyler bites my skin, "What if I let you fuck me here, right here? You'd say no?"

"Let me? If I wanted to fuck you, I would."

"You don't want to?" He presses his thigh between my legs. My building erection is a surprise to me. Tyler chuckles, "Come on, Nick. No lube. Pain and pleasure all rolled into one."

I'm unsure if he's serious, and I'm not sure I wouldn't take him up on the offer. Fucking in the ass, man or woman, feels fantastic, not that I would ever admit that to anyone. The tightness is beyond this world, though I could do without his bony ass. Katie has a perfectly plump tush that jiggles.

I wouldn't mind trying again with Tyler. We fucked a few weeks ago, but I was hurting him, and he wasn't able to cum. Maybe next time we can both get a little drunk, and I won't hurt him so much, and I won't care even if I do.

"You wouldn't be able to take it."

He kisses me, and I forget for a minute I'm at work. I grab the back of his head, our tongues twist, and I can taste the alcohol. Blood rushes to my cock, and I'm wondering when Katie is coming back so we could have a little threesome on my desk.

Tyler backs out, "Damn right about that," he laughs, and I'm shoving him, feeling stupid for getting sucked in. He nearly stumbles back and falls in the chair. "Gonna have to get rid of that," he points to my pants and the apparent lump, "Before you can go out there."

"If I wasn't working, I'd make you fix this."

Two

Nick: Red

When one of my servers comes to me to help her because Tyler has officially grossed out her table, I head over against my better judgment. Tyler stands beside the half-eaten cake, taking a swig of his whiskey before he goes on, "I didn't know what to do. I grabbed my clothes with the ropes still attached to my wrists and ankles and walked out the front door, butt naked."

I slap a hand on his shoulder, and his attention zips to me, "Nick! Dude, I've been looking for you," he wraps an arm around me.

"You're a little loud."

"No, it's alright. But I am hungry."

I sit him down at the table and grab someone's dumplings. He snatches it careless to the cold and stuffs it down. I'm nervous. I don't want him to do anything stupid.

When we are alone, I can handle Tyler. I can deal with the

insinuations. I can tolerate the sexual remarks, his flirtation, and his affection.

It was odd in the beginning. I remember when we first started to explore a bisexual relationship, kissing him was difficult. But now, after years of it, it's natural. Yeah, he's a man, and yeah, it feels different. Sometimes it doesn't feel good at all. Tyler is all muscle, and that's a little off-putting, but I evolved. I forced myself to like it. That might sound bad, but I had to if I wanted to explore more.

And I do want to explore more.

This adventure that we are on has been the most exciting, crazy, exhilarating ride I've ever experienced. Sometimes it's scary, but that's what makes it awesome. How many people out there would have taken this opportunity? Katie, Tyler, and I have broken barriers. We've done things many people will only ever fantasize over. They don't dare do what we are doing.

The only thing stopping me from enjoying it a hundred percent of the time is my faith. Some will tell me to ignore it or forget it, but it's a part of who I am. I can't just stop thinking about God. I have to figure out how to exist with what I'm doing and what I believe in.

Tyler doesn't understand that. He doesn't believe in God, and that's fine. But it makes us fight more than we should because he can't fathom how I'm struggling.

There are days when I'm fine with what we're doing. Then there are days when I can't look at myself in the mirror. I'll figure out a balance soon. Tyler needs to give me time to do it, and that's a problem. He wants it all now, and I can't give it.

Tyler wants to marry me. Crazily, I agreed. Why, if I'm such doubts?

When skydiving, there are a hundred reasons not to do it.

10

But when freefalling, it's exhilarating. When landing, the only thought that remains is, 'I'm fucking happy I did it.'

That's my mentality. I'm currently freefalling, praying I land on my feet.

Marco sits beside us, and I ask him, "Aren't you supposed to be working?"

"Aren't you?" he sarcastically replies. Marco taps Tyler, "So are you gonna answer?"

"Oh, Nick!" Tyler bursts out, "So let me tell you how many people have asked me which one of us takes it in the ass—"

"Ty—"

"It's me! I admit it. I'm so in love with this guy I let him—"

I grip his arm, pulling him close, viciously whispering in his ear, "That's enough."

I see red; everything is fucking red. I can barely breathe as I yank Tyler along, stumbling and cursing as I weave through the restaurant with eyes on us. I shove him into my office, slamming the door shut. He catches himself on the desk, laughing, thinking this is some sort of game.

"What is wrong with you!"

"Relax, bro, no one cared."

"I care. You realize those are my employees. This is my place of business. You want to embarrass me for what reason?"

"Embarrass you? How am I embarrassing you? We are getting married—"

"God!" I'm pacing, and in this small ass office, it just feels like I'm going in circles. I can't believe he said that in front of all our friends. In front of my subordinates. "You aren't happy no matter how much I give, are you? You just fucking take. I'm over it. I'm so fucking over it. Oh my god. Oh god."

"Relax, bro, it was a joke."

"Our life isn't a joke, Tyler. This isn't a joke to me. I'm struggling every day accepting us. I thought if I just forced myself to jump, I'd be okay. But I can't swim any faster. I can't catch up to you quick enough." I hold my head in my hands, trying to think, trying to stop the thoughts rushing through my head. I'm so pissed I just want to punch him in the goddamn face. How could he say it? How could he say it in front of everybody?

Tyler touches my hands, and I snap up, shoving him back, but he holds up his hands, "I'm sorry. I'm sorry, Nick, it was stupid. I was stupid."

I fall back against the door, shaking my head, just staring at him. "I can't do this."

"Can't do what?"

In this moment of clarity, the exact words repeat over and over again: I can't do this. I can't do this.

How do I make him understand? How will Katie understand? Can I back out now? I thought I could be fine. I want to be fine, but I'm not, and Tyler isn't making this easy. He's standing on top of a mountain confessing our life for the world while I'm still climbing, slipping, falling.

"You want more than I can give you."

"What does that mean? Nick, I'm sorry. I'm drunk. I'm stupid when I'm drunk."

"We'll talk later."

I move to go, but he grabs my arm, begging, "No, no, please."

I look at him. He's scared; he's nervous. He's such a little kid when it comes to relationships. I feel like I'm gonna break him.

"I don't think this is gonna work," the words come out, and there's truth in them, but it's mixed in with so many other things.

12

"What? Me and you?"

"Me and you. You and Katie. I don't think I can do it."

Tyler steps back, "Why? Because I spout my mouth off? Really?"

"Yes, and because you said you were in love with me."

His brows knit, "Why did you think I wanted to marry you?"

"I don't know. I don't know. For Katie, maybe? Convenience?"

"Convenience? Is that why you said yes? It was convenient?"

"No—"

"What's convenient about it, Nick? I'm here, so you might as well fuck me too? That's not how it works. You feel something. You're just so ashamed you won't admit it. You're such a fucking pussy."

Tyler shoves me to get out the door, but I push him back, "You run now, I will not chase after you. I didn't mean it, alright? It wasn't convenient. I meant that we were just going with it. I thought we were just going with it. I didn't know that's why you want to marry me. I didn't think it was like that."

"What did 'all in' mean to you?"

I stall in my response. I'm digging a hole for myself. Times where Katie and I fight, and I don't know if I'm right or wrong. "I don't know. More fucking, I guess."

He shakes his head, just staring at me.

I scratch my temple, realizing how bad that sounded. "Look; we'll talk again later. When you're sober."

"I'm fine. I understand just fine. You don't want to do this anymore because you don't love me. At least now I know," he moves for the door, "Tell Katie I'll call her later."

"Where are you going?"

Tyler meets my eye, "I told you in the very beginning if you

13

ever wanted me to go. I'd go. That's what I'm gonna do. Unless you stop me."

He waits.

And I think about it, I really do, but I don't know how I feel, I don't know if it's love. Could I love a man? I don't want to think I can. I don't want to love a man. So I should let him go, right?

He walks out.

A ball of disgust drops into my belly. It only happens to me when I regret something. It's such a rare thing that when I feel it, I know it because it's the worst feeling in the world and impossible to forget.

I was so pissed before. He announced to the whole room I was fucking him in the ass. What did he think I was going to do? Laugh? That wasn't a push from him, that was being hit by a goddamn semi and flying. He had no right to say that. He's so dumb.

Or fearless.

Shit.

What have I done?

Three

Tyler: Hate

❧

I stand in the back of the restaurant, my head thrown back to look at the night sky. I'm leaving. I'm leaving, and I won't let it hurt. This was always going to happen. From the first night where I stayed when I shouldn't have, this was an inevitability.

"Ty, you alright?" a server questions blowing smoke into the air.

"Good," I move toward my car.

Katie will understand. She was always meant for Nick. I was simply an addition, like an added room to a house. But in the original blueprint, I don't exist.

"Tyler."

I'm at my car door when I hear Nick call.

"Jarod, get inside," he sends the server in, leaving us alone.

I rest my hands on the top of the car, closing my eyes, refusing to turn around. I can barely keep the world from spinning, but

I'd much rather risk driving than hear anything else he has to say.

I've screwed up. He wants to break up, and I'm not gonna beg him to stay. He constantly tells me I push too hard. Well, I'm not pushing anymore. I've been trying to get him to ease up, to relax about our lifestyle. I thought if I overcompensated with how easy it is, he'd follow suit, but instead, I've ruined everything.

Maybe this is what my dad goes on about. I'm messed up on some deeper level that only he sees. It's suddenly made very clear why he thinks I need help. I self-destruct even when I'm not trying to.

"Hey," It's a different voice, and on the other side of the car, there is a group of guys heading toward us. "Are you Tyler and Nick?"

Nick greets them, "How can we help you, gentlemen?"

"Take your bitch and get out of the city."

"What?"

The stranger punches Nick, and he falls against the car.

I struggle to process what's happening, and by the time I realize this is an ambush, another douchebag comes around and throws a sudden punch that knocks me to the ground. I shuffle to my feet, a bit unsteady, wiping blood from my eye. I'm backing up, not ready to fight, in no mood to fight a stranger for whatever reason they have. When he goes to punch again, I'm a little more prepared, and I duck and dive into him, crashing us to the floor. I'm on my feet quickly, running to help Nick. He's being kicked and punched by two guys. He tries to protect himself, arms covering his head, but every punch gets his ribs and shoulders hit. I pile drive into them, knocking them to the floor. I scrap a knee, an elbow, but the pain is numb, the alcohol protecting me.

I get to my feet and kick one of them in the ribs. The other gets up, backing up, a bit more afraid now that I'm fighting back. An unseen third one slams a fist into my temple. I drop to the ground so fucking hard I almost lose consciousness.

"Fucking fag."

I curl into the ground, the dizziness to the point of nausea. I repeatedly blink to clear my head, but I can't recover fast enough as the three of them attack. The first to the ribs, the second to the back, another kicks at my legs. "Get up, fairy. Or maybe you like being on the bottom." A kick to the face lands me on my back, and they take shots, pounding my ribs in. No matter how I try to protect myself, there's another one hitting me somewhere else.

Then Nick runs into two of them, allowing me to deal with the third. I grab his foot, twisting it, and he falls to the floor. I keep turning, hoping to break his foot. He punches me in the back of the head, and I release him, holding my head. I'm so tired and dizzy, but I can't stop. Nick's around here somewhere, and I have to help.

I'm trying to get up. I can't see; there's blood in my eye. I can barely breathe. Hot pain envelops my ribs as I roll over.

I'm up on my knees, searching for Nick. It's dark, with a random street light far off. One of the guys is barely conscious on the floor. Nick has the other against the wall, pounding his fists into their face. The stranger drops to the ground, and Nick is panting, backing up. It would be a victory, except he's forgotten about the third one.

I crawl, half stumbling, "Nick!"

The third one shoves a knife into his back.

Nick drops to the floor, crying out. Life seems to stall as I struggle to get to my feet. It's quiet and yet piercing. I meet his eyes from across the way, full of shock, full of fear that it pushes me up. The group attacking us disappears just as quickly as they had come.

I limp to his side, falling on my knees beside him, gripping his hand.

"It's fine." He assures me. "It's fine. I'm fine."

"Yeah, Yeah, you're fine," I reply automatically. "Let me look." Using my phone for light, I lift his shirt to look at it.

A small tear in his back leaks dark blood. If the knife managed to puncture his kidney, he'd bleed out before the ambulance arrived. I drop the phone and take off my shirt. "Pressure. Hold it, as hard as you can."

"Um-hm."

My hands are shaking as I dial 911. The screen is shattered, and there is blood on my fingers, but I manage it. "I need an ambulance in the back at the Flesh restaurant downtown. My my my friend's been stabbed. He's bleeding; please hurry."

I drop the phone on the floor; the woman remains on speaker, telling me help is on the way. "Try not to move. I'm gonna put more pressure. It's gonna hurt."

"How bad is it?"

Despite panicking, knowing all the percentages and things that could go wrong, I shrug as I press all my weight onto the wound, "Flesh wound."

He groans, "Liar. Worst pain of my life."

"Try getting it in the ass."

Nick snorts and then winces, "Ah shit, don't make me laugh."

Four

Tyler: Stay

❧

The ambulance doors open up, and the EMTs pull out the gurney. My bloody hand slips from Nick's, and they are rolling him inside. I stand there glued to the spot as the doctors and nurses converge around him. He disappears inside, the doors silent as they shut.

Katie slams into me, hugging me sloppily before she chases after the medical team.

It felt like hours in that ambulance, but it was only minutes. I stare down at my bloody arms and fingers. The amount of blood Nick lost was substantial. It seemed no matter how much pressure I put on it; it just kept coming. He would be okay. Nick was a beast, and nothing could bring him down. I have no doubt he will recover. It's what makes it easy to walk away.

Now's the time when no one is looking or paying attention. Now's my chance to leave.

I always knew when it was the perfect moment to get out of relationships. I don't know why it's been a knack of mine since I started as an escort. You learn quickly you don't want to deal with any drama or clinging clients, so I'm out the door and down the street before they even get a chance.

You don't look back. You don't hesitate or stumble. You leave like it's the easiest thing in the whole fucking world.

David and Ray get out of the car, and though they try to reach me, I don't hear it. I keep walking. One foot in front of the other. It's how it should have been. It's how it was always going to be. I had no place here. I should have never stayed the night.

But I stumble, and I wrap an arm around my chest, smearing blood over my skin in a silly attempt to ease the pain. It's like breathing fire. I can't take full breaths, and I know something is broken.

But it doesn't matter.

I keep moving.

I got to keep moving.

"Hey!"

I close my eyes when Katie sounds. She wasn't supposed to come back out. I was supposed to have a clean getaway with no fucking tears or stupid ass arguments. This isn't something that can be won. She'll have to face it like I'm doing.

Her footsteps pound the pavement as she chases me, and she jumps in front of me teary-eyed and wildly afraid. "Where the hell do you think you're going?"

I can't think. My brain is made of marbles, and every move I make shakes them around, scrambling any thoughts.

She shoves me, "You gonna run? Are fucking kidding me?"

How can I tell her that we're over? Will she accept it? Would she believe me? Nick and I tried to make it work, but we're too different. Katie doesn't know about our attempts at a relationship. She won't understand why I'm leaving, but it's better this way. For some fucking reason.

She shoves me again, "I don't give a fuck if this has to do with your mom; you are going in that hospital. Go. Nick needs you!" She pushes me and smacks me. Then she falls against me with her head on my chest, "I need you. Stay. Please stay."

Her pitiful voice pulls at me. I can't hurt her. Not purposely. I close my eyes, hoping to find some strength to keep going, to leave now while everything is chaotic, but she weighs me down.

I wrap my arms around her, burying my face into her hair. She clings to me, and it feels like I'm gonna break—my body trembles. The pain is building with every passing second. My adrenaline is running out.

I don't know when it transforms, but instead of me comforting her, she's comforting me. "It's alright," she whispers. "You have to let the doctor see you, okay? You're hurt. You're bleeding. Please."

With an arm around her shoulder, she leads me back to the hospital, where a nurse is waiting to take me to the ER. Another nurse takes Katie to an area where she can wait for Nick. David goes with her while my brother Ray stays with me.

It's a rush of questions, of movement that I don't pay attention. Ray answers the questions that I can't. I'm having trouble concentrating. All the movement, the nurses, and the smells brought me back years ago when I was wheeled into the hospital with a piece of glass sticking out of my chest. The lights are the same. The ceiling is as it was years ago.

"Adam," Ray calls.

His voice sounds like Dad. My dad was beside me in my

memory, whispering words of encouragement, telling me I was strong and I'll make it through. While all I kept thinking about was my dead mother sitting beside in the driver's seat with a blanket pulled over her face.

I close my eyes at some point, and sleep takes over.

* * *

I wash my hands. It's a simple action, something that I can do in my sleep. Scrub the palms. Between the fingers. On the backside. Past the wrist. Round and round. Repeat.

Repeat.

Repeat.

"Tyler."

I flinch, lifting my eyes. The mirror shows my reflection. Bruises shine on both eyes with a bit of swelling. A busted lips. Blood dried on my temple-gauze over my eyebrow.

All of Nick's blood washed away, leaving behind substantial black and purple welts on my chest, ribs, and back. There are a few cuts and scrapes along my arms and legs that have been cleaned and bandaged.

Ray shuts off the water, "Come on, let me get you back."

I move to follow him, but the action is hard, and I grip his arm to keep steady. Three broken ribs send ripples of agony through my entire chest. Every move is brutal. The bruising and headache are only small additions and are barely recognized.

Ray directs me back to the gurney bed, helping me up, and replacing the ice packs to my stomach and face.

"Can't he get anything?" he pleads to the nurse.

"He's still working off his liquor. As soon as he blows below a .01, I'll give him something."

"That will take hours. He's not a drunk or a pill popper. He was just viciously attacked!"

"Ray."

Ray clamps his lips, gripping the bed sheets.

"I'm okay."

He hangs his head, trying to hide his face. "This is ridiculous."

"I don't know. If I can handle a speech right now, bro."

He chuckles forcefully, "I'm not mad at you. What gives anyone the right to do this?" His voice breaks, and he bows his head. "When that ambulance showed up, I knew it was you. Like the job wasn't finished or something."

I hold up my hand, and he takes it, resting his forehead on it. "I'm good, bro. I'm not going anywhere."

He nods, "Shit, I'll be back," his voice breaks as he rushes away.

I stare at the ceiling. I never thought about what the car accident was like for Ray. I guess I'm not the only one fucked up from it.

The nurse pulls a blanket over me, "Try to sleep."

"Where's Nick?"

"I told you as soon as I know anything, so will you."

"Where's Katie?"

"I told you, she went to talk to Nick's parents. You have a slight concussion. Try to rest."

"I'm thirsty."

"I already brought you some water, honey."

* * *

It could be seconds, minutes, hours; I have no track of time.

My eyes snap open, and a doctor is standing in front of me. But he's not looking at me. He's talking over me, through me. I'm too tired to care. My head hurts too much to concentrate.

"What does that mean?" Ray asks.

"He needs to contact his cardiologist and get on medication to help manage it. Considering the damage that was done in the car accident, I can't believe he hasn't been on anything. He's been fortunate so far."

"But. He hasn't had any symptoms. He tells me everything. He's never complained about any of it."

"He's young and fit. Works out. He probably didn't notice it or thought it was normal. Like I said, we caught it early. He's very lucky despite the circumstances."

I touch Ray's arm. It feels like a dream. I tap on his shoulder, "I'm okay."

"Adam. Did you know about this?"

"About what?"

"I'll come back in the morning. He has a concussion, so temporary memory loss and confusion are common. It should be better in a few hours. Once we get back the final tests, he can go home. As long as he promises to call his cardiologist."

I look at Ray. His face is full of concern, and he just stares into space. I pull at his shirt. "I'm good, man."

"How is this 'good', Adam? Heart Failure? It's this life. It's stressful. It's not worth it."

"Heart Failure?"

He pats me on the shoulder, "Rest. I'm gonna call dad."

"You should go home. I'll call you tomorrow."

"Alright. Love you, bro."

"You too," I watch him go, but I can't keep my eyes open long enough.

* * *

I jump up, panicked, pain in every part of my body. I hold my head, but dizziness drops me back to the bed.

"Hey." David lays a hand on my shoulder, "You're alright. Relax."

"Where am I?"

David laughs, "Really? We've been talking for like ten minutes."

"Sorry."

"You're at the hospital. You were attacked outside the restaurant."

"Why?"

He pauses, maybe trying to figure out if he should tell me, then he shrugs, "Dicks."

"Where's Nick? He was hurt, wasn't he?"

"Yeah."

I look at my hands. They're clean, but I specifically remember blood. In the crusts of my nails is the only evidence. I must have cleaned my hands already. I tug at my shirt, "This yours?"

"Yeah, I had an extra one."

"Oh, good. I was hoping I didn't have such bad taste."

He cracks a laugh, "Screw you."

I close my eyes again.

"Tyler?"

My brows knit, "Why are you calling me by my escort name? Don't tell me you're a client."

He looks up, "See? He keeps going back and forth."

"It's the concussion," the nurse assures, "Memory loss is common, but it's temporary. Don't worry. We did a CT Scan."

"I'm good," I reassure him. "I just forgot for a minute."

25

"What's my name?"

I chuckle, "Testing me?" I open my eyes and look at him. It takes a while for the connection to work before it clicks again, "David. See?"

"Alright. You thirsty?"

"Is Nick okay? He was hurt. Wasn't he?"

"He just got out of surgery. He's in recovery. My sister's there."

"Is he okay?"

He pauses, and it freaks me out. I try to sit up, but he keeps me down. "He lost his kidney."

I clench my eyes shut, cursing, falling against the table.

"But he's alive. He'll live. And it's because of you."

I'm about to ask what happened when memories surface. I stare off, watching it again and again.

"They called me a fag."

David's brows knit in a sadness, "I'm sorry, man."

* * *

Opening my eyes once more, I hear crying.

I turn my head, and a brunette woman lays with her head on my arm. I reach over; the move, however, is too painful. A groan gets her attention instead. "Hey, beautiful."

She stands quickly, her brown eyes bloodshot and her face wet with tears, "Hey, honey."

"I probably should know you."

Her brows knit in concern, "You have a concussion."

"I figured it was something."

"The nurse was finally able to give you something. You were drinking, and they wouldn't give you anything."

26

I smile, "Sounds about right. We fucking or are you a client?"

The pain in her face recedes. She bites her lip like a sex kitten and reveals, "We're getting married."

My brows rise as I meet her reassuring grin. "Wow." I look over her once more. "I got lucky, huh?"

"No, baby. I did." She touches my face, her finger dancing on my jaw. The way she looks at me is unlike anyone who has ever looked at me. I realize then what it is: Love. I didn't think I would ever find anyone to love me. Her expression changes into concern, "Are you in any pain?"

I shake my head for a moment, unable to speak as I look her over. Then I smirk, "I know why I love you."

"Oh yeah, already?"

"Your tits."

She busts out laughing, kissing my cheek. "Even when you don't know what's going on, you're still a charmer."

"Show me a tittie. Come on. I've never seen them before."

"Oh Tyler, you are—"

Confusion makes me interrupt. "That's my escort name."

"Oh god, I can't stop myself. You want to know something else?" She leans and whispers, "You were fucked by my husband."

I think about it for a minute, then shrug, "Not too surprising, I guess. I've done some crazy shit."

"Oh, I know."

"Never thought I'd go there, though. You must be some fine ass pussy for me to go that far."

She laughs again, and I love the sound. I admire the way she moves; her hair seems to fall so perfectly down her face. Even a complete wreck, she is beautiful. She smiles through her evident sadness.

27

"So what happened?"

"You were attacked."

"Are you okay?"

"Yeah, I wasn't there. Nick was. He's in recovery. The doctor told me that you saved his life."

"You know I'm going to be a doctor, so it only seems right. I got like four more years to go."

"Oh no, darling, you are all done. Tonight was your congratulatory party."

"No way."

"Totally," she mocks with a smile.

"So I finished. Man, I like this future. Well, aside from getting fucked in the ass by a man." I make her laugh again, and the sound is harmony in my ears.

Five

Tyler: Control

⟨ornament⟩

The hospital released me in the morning. My head pounds with every step, but at least my memories returned. My body looks like I've been hit by a truck, and it feels like that too. Even my fingers hurt. I think the only part of me that's not in pain is my toes.

I toss my release papers into the trash can, unwilling to take the risk anyone finds them. We have enough going on without worrying about stupid shit. My cardiologist, after the accident, always told me something would happen. Not could, but would. He told me to pay attention to signs of heart failure or the eighty other problems that could occur. I thought if I kept a good exercise routine, ate healthily, and stayed away from drugs, I'd be alright. But I can't fight age.

Heart failure is treatable. It may not have a cure, but I can be fine for a long time without problems. I'll need some medication. I'll have to stay away from stressful situations, which is more of a problem than I realized. Otherwise, I should be good for a while. It's nothing that needs immediate attention, so for now, I'll keep it to myself.

All I want to do is go home and fall in bed, but I head to Nick's room. I still haven't seen him, and though our last conversation repeats in my head, I want to see him. Everyone has told me he's okay, but I need to find out for myself, so I'm weaving through the corridors trying to find my way to Ortho. I've been to this hospital plenty of times during my schooling. I love the smell of hospitals. It's clean and fresh despite all the disease and death. I have a little morbidity to me, but I'm planning on being a surgeon, so death has to fascinate me on some level.

Though Katie seemed to think my mother was the reason I didn't chase after Nick, hospitals feel more like home. I did my clinicals here. I've followed doctors around for hours at a time. I've worn a doctor's coat. I'm ready to step into the shoes I've always wanted.

The hospital isn't the trigger for my mother. She died in a car anyway; if nothing else, it should have been the car. But for me, the trigger is the chance of losing someone that I love. And Nick is one of those people. I don't know what it will be like seeing him, and I don't know how to prepare.

But like all things, it's better to rip it off like a bandaid. Sirens are going off in my brain to run away as I push open the door with all sense of bravado.

Katie is in a chair beside him, half asleep. She pops her head up upon seeing me and forces a weak, tired smile, "How are you feeling?"

I shrug, "About as good as I look."

Nick is between us asleep, and all I do is stare.

She gives a fake chuckle, "Not good then."

He's only got a bruise on his cheek, a much better face than my own. But he has a broken finger, and his knuckles on both fists are wrapped up in gauze. He looks white, and for a naturally tanned Spanish man, it's overwhelming. He appears feeble. He looks old.

I lean back against the wall, blinking rapidly, chewing on my lip, trying not to allow all the damn emotions to breakthrough. I'm so angry at everything, at everyone, at those fucking dipshits that attacked us. I'm mad at Nick for splitting up with me over something so stupid. I don't even know if I should be here. But how can I leave? I love him.

I turn, facing the wall, punching it, taking out all my aggression on the brick. I've never been so angry, and I don't know where to put it. I don't know how to shove it down. It's boiling over, and there is no way to turn down the heat. Blood breaks through my skin, and the white concrete turns red. I want their faces. I want their fear to replace mine.

Katie rushes to my side, intervening. She's grabbing my face, "It's okay, I'm so sorry, baby. I'm so sorry."

I squeeze my eyes shut, and I cling to Katie, burying my face in her neck.

* * *

The nurse wakes us up, apologizing as he wheels in his kit. I sit in the corner while Katie lays out on the couch. He wakes up Nick, and for the first time, I hear Nick's voice, "I'm hungry." He announces.

He can't see me as he talks to the nurse, asking random questions and telling random jokes that make the nurse laugh. Just listening to him, it's like home. He's normal despite the trauma that's happened. It's like another day in the office. He's fine, and I don't know how he does it. I don't feel fine. I feel betrayed. I want revenge, but on who? I know their faces, but I don't know who they are.

Katie gets up, and Nick greets her, "Hey, baby, why haven't you gone home?"

"I told you I'm not going anywhere. Are you in pain?"

"Not really. These drugs must be good. Hey, where's Tyler?"

I get up unsteadily, and the movement brings his attention to me. His eyes widen. "Oh God."

"I'm okay."

He curses as he tries to get up, but the nurse holds his shoulder, keeping him down, "Not so fast, cowboy."

"Those sons of a bitches. I'm gonna kill them. I'm gonna kill them, I swear to God." He clenches his eyes shut, holding his side. A wave of pain knocking out his anger and good mood. He pants to calm the pain.

The nurse changes the subject by getting Nick to eat, using the bathroom, and brushing his teeth. It takes a lot of coaxing from Katie and the nurse while I sit back and watch. Nick's a pretty easy-going guy, but when in pain, he's a freaking baby. He's combative, argumentative, and completely uncooperative. I wouldn't have thought that about him, but then again, he's never been hurt the whole time I've known him.

A knock on the door and the doctor walks in, "Oh good; you're up. How are you feeling?"

"Like I got stabbed, how do you want me to feel?"

"Nick," Katie chastises.

He holds up a hand, "Sorry. It just hurts."

"Well, we can up your pain medicine for a bit, but the key is walking. Let's take a look. Despite losing a kidney, you were fortunate your friend was there. With stab wounds, blood loss is usually significant."

Despite him meaning well, it pisses me off. I'm the reason Nick was a target to begin with. If I didn't exist, he would have never been stabbed.

Nick jokes, "Guess all the money toward your schooling worked out."

I'm not in any mood for fucking jokes. I stay quiet as the doctor goes about talking about his recovery process. Six weeks of no strenuous activity, including sex, and Nick has plenty to say, making Katie and the doctor laugh. I hate it. Why is he acting like this isn't a big fucking deal? How can his pride still be intact? Mine is in shreds. I should have been able to beat the shit out of those fucks. Instead, I feel like a dork that got caught on the football field.

When the nurse and doctor leave, Nick's attention reverts to me, "What's up with you? Why are you over there pouting?"

"Pouting?"

Not only is he gonna act like we didn't just get jumped, but is he gonna pretend he didn't break up with me too?

"Yeah, you got a moody face on."

I scoff, shaking my head. I glance to the door, really fighting the urge to walk out.

Nick notices it. "Surprised you're here, thought you'd be halfway to Mexico by now—"

"You know—"

"Tyler," Katie cuts in, "He's joking with you."

I run my hand through my hair, trying to calm the overwhelming rage. It's not like me, and I hate how much it's taking over. I'm usually in way more control than this, but I feel like I have no control over anything.

I don't have control over Nick.

I don't have control over strangers.

I don't have control over the uselessness of my body.

I'm spiraling, and escape is my main priority.

Six

Tyler: Secret

A knock on the door wakes me. I'm laid out on the couch, and at some point, Katie put a blanket over me. I don't want to move because for a few seconds now, I've been pain-free. But it doesn't last. I struggle sitting up, and Katie has to help. My ribs are on fire. She is quick to bring me pain pills and water.

A police officer walks in. "Hey, Nick."

Katie and I glance at one another. Since when does Nick know a cop?

"Hey, Chris."

"How are you feeling?"

"Ahh. Been better."

The police officer points at me, "You're Tyler? You talked to someone, right?"

I shrug, "Probably, I don't know; everything is pretty much a blur."

"We're gonna need a statement, and the more you remember, the better. I got some good news for you, gentlemen. We got one of the guys that attacked you. Thanks to your security footage. He's been on our list for a while. Attack another gay couple a few months ago, but he got bailed out."

"Well, that's good, I guess."

"But it is what we suspected. The AFA."

Nick nods as if that word makes any sense.

Katie inquires, "The AFA?"

"American Family Association." The police officer explains. "They are a large hate group here in Pennsylvania. With all the hate letters and vandalism, we thought it was only a matter of time before it escalated."

Katie and I both look at Nick, but he avoids us.

"Pressing charges may sound good, but be prepared; it might get worse. We can keep a cop outside your house and your job, but I don't know for how long. I'll talk to my supervisor, see what we can do."

They talk a little bit more than shake hands, and the cop is out the door. Katie stands next to him, obviously fuming. I sit back and let her handle it. She's sexy as hell when she's screaming at someone else.

"When the hell were you going to tell me?"

"I wasn't planning to. You were already stressed—"

"I'm not a weak fucking bitch that can't handle it. Don't you treat me like some little girl. I am your wife. We are equal. I deserved to know. Tyler deserved to know."

"Like I said, I didn't think it would escalate. I thought it was stupid kids. Now I know better. I'll start carrying—"

"Carrying what? A gun, are you serious?" Katie looks toward

me, maybe hoping for support, but I'm on Nick's side with this.

"Despite what you think," Nick says, "a gun could have actually stopped this. I could have saved us both. Instead, Tyler looks like he got run over, and I lost half my blood supply. What if you had been there and I couldn't protect you? Look at Tyler; you want to look like that?"

"So you plan on killing someone? What's God have to say about that?"

"I'm allowed to protect myself and my family. If you think I'll just stand by and let this happen again, you don't know me."

"Maybe your father can talk some sense into you," she heads out.

"He'll agree with me!" Nick shouts after her.

I get up and leave. I don't want to be left alone with him lest he provokes me into an argument. Despite being pissed he kept it from us, I'm about to do the same damn thing. I'm a hypocrite, keeping my illness a secret. I have no room to be upset.

I think about telling Katie, so I'm not in the same boat as Nick. I follow her to the waiting room where his parents sit, drinking coffee, reading the newspaper. She's ranting in front of them, pacing, and they simply sit and watch her like she's a TV show.

I can wait.

* * *

I stand in front of the vending machine, spaced out, blindly staring, trying to figure out what Katie would like to eat. Katie's very picky when it comes to food. She eats the same meal everywhere we go. I can't remember what chips she likes. If

Nick were here, he'd know. He knows everything about her. I can never match up to him. I should be the one in bed. I'm the one that the mob should have stabbed.

I rub my eyes. I'm tired. I'm tired of being tired.

"Hey."

I glance vaguely as Martin stands beside me. "Hey."

Martin, Nick's older brother, and myself have never gotten along. Aside from him trying to rape Katie a few years ago, he's a fucking bigot. But we've managed a false amicable relationship in recent months. He isn't as much of a dick, and I'm not picking fights. That being said, this is only our second time around each other since January, so we haven't had much practice.

"I heard you saved Nick's life."

I push a button, "I didn't do shit."

"We agree on something."

I wince, leaning down to crap the bag of chips. Here I thought Martin was gonna thank me. It would have been out of his character, so I shouldn't be surprised.

"See," he goes on, "Got to think, who put him in that position to begin with? Can't be considered a saint when you're to blame."

"Speaking of positions, when Nick and I are fucking, he really likes—"

"Okay, guys," David steps between us, taping Martin on the shoulder, "Nick's awake, asking for you."

Martin doesn't take his eyes off me as he backs up. I can't stop my smirk, knowing he'd never attack with innocent little David between us. Martin nods, as if he's figured me out and takes off.

David looks at me with annoyance, "I see why Nick gets

pissed at you."

"He was asking for it."

"Maybe, but that's his brother. Then last night at the party. I didn't know Nick could get so mad. You do it on purpose. I don't get you."

I avoid him, pissed at myself and pissed at the fucking world. "You might not have to wonder about it for too long. Nick broke things off last night."

"If my girlfriend embarrassed me like that I would too. But it would be momentary. I'm sure he doesn't feel that way now."

I shrug, dropping in a chair, staring at the bag of chips in my hands. Does Katie even like these?

David sits beside me, "Have you told them yet? About what the doctor said. Heart Failure."

I throw my head back. I didn't think anyone knew. "Who told you?"

"Ray."

I blow out air, trying to come up with some excuse. At least now I know Ray knows. I can stop him from telling anyone. Especially my father. "I'm fine."

"Sure. Now. But without treatment, you'll get worse."

"I'll take care of it."

"If you don't tell her, I will."

I roll my eyes, "Thought you were my friend."

"I am your friend. But I'm Katie's brother first."

"Just give me a few days. I can't really think right now."

"It's been a rough day. It would help if you ate something better than chips. I'll go out. Get some food for you guys. You guys like McDonald's?"

"Burger King. A stacker. Dr. Pepper. For both."

"Alright. I'm gonna let your dog out too. Get you some

clothes. I know how much you love my shirt."

I get up with him, smacking his hand, hugging him quickly, "Thanks, David."

"Stick around, Ty. Give Nick some time, and I'm sure you guys will make up."

"Why are you sure?"

David smiles, "Just am."

I sit back down and stare blankly at the floor. I'm too tired to think, to feel, to figure out what the hell I'm supposed to do. The problems are piling on. I don't want to think about this bullshit diagnosis. It's not real yet.

My attention, my mind, keeps going back to the ambush.

How can I fight back? I can't fight a whole organization. I was better knowing it was just a couple of homophobic assholes. There has to be some other reason other than our relationship. Did I do something stupid to them? Did I insult them? It's not so far-fetched to believe because I do stupid shit all the time. It has to be my fault. I'm constantly pushing Nick to be more physical in public.

Even if Nick hadn't broken up with me last night, I'd contemplate leaving. What if I stay and this happens again? What if Katie is there next time? Nick's right; how would I be able to protect her when I failed so badly at protecting him? I should have fought better.

Is this relationship even worth the trouble?

Seven

Tyler: Time

❧❧❧

"I'm fine, dad."

Ray got to my dad before I could stop him. Now I have to sit and listen to another lecture. It's been going on for several minutes. He's on repeat mode, acting as if he says it enough times; I'll actually listen.

"You were told this could happen. Now you need to come home. I'll take care of you."

"I'm not fifteen anymore. Would you stop?"

"Adam, if you don't take this seriously, you're gonna end up needing a new heart. Who's gonna give you a heart? You're an alcoholic prostitute."

"I'm a doctor."

"You should have listened to Dr. Hills. Stress will kill you. You were lucky to survive that crash. You need to be careful."

"I gotta go."

I struggle to hit the off button with my screen shattered, and even as I attempt, I can still hear him talking, trying to convince me to come home. I'm about to throw it in the trash when it finally beeps and shuts him off.

I head back to the room just as Martin is coming out. He doesn't say anything to me; our game at being friends on pause. I walk in to find Nick sitting up, eating pudding.

"Where's Katie?"

"Fresh air."

Martin probably said something to piss her off.

"I'll go find her."

"Tyler."

I hesitate in the doorway, clinging to the knob.

"Anything broken?"

"Three of my ribs." I hold up my newly bandaged hand, "Hairline fracture." At least they cleaned the blood off the wall.

"Come here."

I clench my teeth, looking down the hall, knowing I can walk away and he can't follow me.

"Get over here."

I shut the door and move to the bed. I don't look at him. I screw up all the time, and I know what he's going to say.

"God, your face. It looks like your pimp fucked you up."

"I would never have a pimp."

He chuckles and lifts a finger, "You got stitches?'

I touch the gauze on my brow, "Just a few. A sucker punch that dropped me to the floor. Slight concussion."

Nick shakes his head quietly. There is no emotion on his face, perhaps too tired to express anything. I want to know what he's thinking. How much does he blame me? Should I go regardless because how can I stay knowing he doesn't want me around? I need him to talk to me because I'm going insane.

"That was some crazy shit. I've never fought like that before."

"You were a beast."

"I wasn't bad. Thought you would do a little better."

"I *was* drunk, asshole. Wasn't really ready for a bunch of homophobic dicks to attack us, either."

My inability to meet his eye becomes obvious, and Nick wheels the tray off his lap. "Sit down."

I sit, but I keep my face turned away. I'm having a terrible time suppressing all my girlish emotions. I'm angry. I'm tired. I'm guilty. I'm overwhelmed with stress and regret.

His hand drops on my thigh. Why touch me if he doesn't want me?

"Don't think any of this is your fault. Katie was going on and on about it being her fault while you were out. So if you think that too, don't."

I hate that he stacks me up against Katie but aren't I the girl in this fucked up relationship that we have? Of course, he's going to treat me like that. And the worst part about it is I need that assurance because that's all I've been thinking.

My teeth clench to hold back any stupid tears. "It is, though. The AFA only attacked us because I'm vocal about everything. Probably pissed one of them off at the restaurant. I'm a fucking loudmouth. You never wanted this. You have always tried to keep me quiet, and I never listened—"

"Ty—"

"I'm always fucking things up. My dad's right. I'm a fucking shitshow."

"No—"

"I nearly got you killed because I don't know how to shut my fucking mouth."

"Would you let me talk!"

"See! I'm doing it now."

I rub my cheek off on my sleeve.

"Whose shirt is this?"

I pull at the fabric, looking at it just for a distraction, "It's David's."

It's quiet after that. I know I have to bring up our conversation before the brawl, but I'm afraid to. I'm worried Nick's only going to reiterate what he already said, and my life is going to blow up in my face.

"About last night,"

"Look, it's fine." I interrupt, standing, unwilling to hear it again. "I can go. Tell Katie I just took off. Put it on me."

"I don't want you to go."

I snap my head to him, confused, "What?"

Nick's tired and rests his head against the pillow; he takes another breath in and admits, "I should have stopped you. I'm sorry, okay?"

I chew on the inside of my lip, staring at him, wondering if he's saying this for me, for Katie, or for himself. Should I just let it go? A part of me wants too. I want to shove it under the rug like we do with a whole ton of shit, but I can't. How can I with everything that he said last night? How can I after he nearly lost his life for what we're doing?

"Can we move on? I mean, in my defense, you did tell everyone I fucked you in the ass—"

"Do you love me?"

His brows knit, "What?"

"I thought we were the same. I thought when you said 'all in' that we were doing this for the right reasons."

"I told you I didn't mean the convenient part."

44

"And what about how I take more than you can give. You mean that?" I wait for a reply, searching his face.

Nick struggles with every word, "You just want everything now."

"What's wrong with that?"

"I can't…" Nick cuts himself off and throws a hand up in the air, giving up.

"Since you can't talk, I'll do it. I love you, Nick. It's different. It's not how I love Katie, but it's fucking close. I want to marry you to be with you. I'm sure you don't want to hear that, but it's the truth."

I'm shaking.

I can't believe I just admitted that. I didn't think those words would ever come out.

He shakes his head, staring at the ceiling.

"So I need to know. Do you love me? It's a yes or no answer. You don't have to say the words. Nod or shake your head. I can't make it any easier."

"Why isn't it enough? What I'm doing?"

"You nearly died. It's not enough, just wanting me around."

"That's not—" He grits his teeth, staring at me. He wants to say something, but he still doesn't have the courage. I know it's hard, but if I was able to say it, he should be able to. Unless it's not what I want to hear, and he's afraid to hurt me.

"I just need time."

I don't know what else to do. I'm struggling because it feels like it's over, and I'm fucking breaking. "You know, I told you," I clear my throat and start again. "Two years ago, I told you I wanted more. Two years, I've been waiting."

Time doesn't seem like too much to ask for. But it's not about the hours and days, weeks and years. It's about how much

45

suffering I'm doing while I wait. While we pretend everything's perfect when it's not. When I don't know if he could ever feel for me the way I do for him.

It didn't bother me until today. Until I nearly lost him for being what we are.

"I'm gonna go for a walk."

"Tyler."

I shut the door behind me.

Eight

Tyler: Teach Me

~~~~~~~~

I've no choice but to put distance between myself and Nick. It's easy to do with him at the hospital. Every day Katie attempts to bring me back, but I manage some excuse. I've been sleeping most of it, enjoying being lazy and careless for once. My body needs to heal; doing anything takes effort.

With Snowball resting on my legs, I watch the sunset from my bed. I've decided that no matter the verdict, my real reason for being here is Katie. Nick was a bonus, but he isn't the end-all to our relationship. I don't need him to be in love with Katie.

It just would have been...

It doesn't matter what it would have been. He doesn't love me, and I'm going to face that. I can stuff my emotions down. I've been doing it ever since I lost my mother. I know how to do it. So why is it so hard?

For the better half of my life, I avoided stress and drama. I hate dealing with all this bullshit. I wanted a simple life, not having to worry about anyone else or anything else. But then I met Katie, and no matter how crazy it got, she was the reason to stay. She *is* the reason to stay.

There's a stigma out there that once you find love, all answers to life's problems are found, and from then on, you are happy. But relationships are complicated and sometimes not fun and definitely not happy. These are the parts that I ran from. But nearly for three years now, I've been training myself to stay. Staying means feeling, and therefore, I've screwed myself. I can't feel 'nothing' anymore. They've changed me, and I don't know if it's necessary for the better. Life without them would be easier.

But not what it could be.

I attempt to roll on my belly, but the pain is too much, and I stay on my side. The pillow smells like Katie, but distantly, Nick's scent is there too. I throw it, grab another, and stuff it under my head.

If I'm going to stay knowing that Nick doesn't love me, could we be friends?

Everyone who's anyone would laugh and tell me 'no'. It's like wanting to be on the beach without the sand. It's impossible to have Katie without Nick. It would never work. It's why it hasn't worked since the beginning. Nick and I were only fighting the inevitable. I gave up quicker than he did.

Is that the answer? Wait him out till he gives up fighting against the unavoidable? Is that the kind of love I want? As he put, 'Convenient'?

Katie is calling. I can go to the hospital for an hour, if only to get her off my back.

* * *

When I get there, the nurse is in. Nick lays on his side while she redoes his bandage. Katie gets up to greet me. She is gentle in her hug, touching my face, asking me how I'm feeling. I've gotten used to the dull ache that seems to encompass my entire body. Only when I breathe is there sharp agony, but it's momentary. It's like being stabbed with a needle every two seconds.

"Hey," Nick greets, "Where you been?"

"Out. Got a new phone. How you doing?"

The nurse answers, "He's almost out of here. Everything is healing great, Nick."

"Good, thank you, DeDe," he rolls on his back, groaning.

"Oh, it's seven o'clock. You want me to turn it on?"

"No-"

"Yes!" Katie eagerly announces, sitting next to me. "A news reporter came to talk to me. She had covered the attack the first night, but now she wants to do a follow-up story. She seemed interested in our situation."

The nurse clicks on the TV, and we watch PA News. Shortly our story comes on the screen. "White supremacists attacks polygamy family."

"Oh god," Nick groans.

"Four days ago, two bisexual men were attacked behind a restaurant for their orientation. It left one of them without a kidney and the other with a concussion and bruises all over his body. This was a serious assault, and two of their assailants are still at large."

They show video footage, and I close my eyes. I can't watch it.

49

I live it every fucking day. Katie rubs my back, whispering an apology. My heart pounds, and every moment of that horrible ambush repeats.

"One man, currently wanted, is seen here. The footage isn't clear enough, but right here, he stabs Mr. Mendez. There is a reward for any information. Hank Mills, the only one of the three arrested, is a known member of the American Family Association, a large hate group in Pennsylvania. And though the AFA has not taken responsibility for the attack, it is not unlikely. If you see or know anything, do not take it into your hands. These men are considered dangerous. Now, as far as reports go, the Mendez family are sweet loving people. They live their lives privately, never pushing their own beliefs on others. Mr. Mendez is the owner of Flesh, a popular restaurant that won the James Beard Award for best new restaurant four years ago. It has become a staple for our community. Customers and co-workers alike were astounded to learn of this horrible assault."

Nick curses, "This is bullshit."

I defend, "This is good, Nick. It's protection."

"My gun is my protection."

Katie nips, "You going to kill someone?"

"Them or me, which would you prefer?"

She scoffs.

The report goes on. "There have been large amounts of support from the LGBT community."

Marco is on the mic, "We have just as much right to be here as anyone else! They don't scare me. I exist!"

The reporter smartly eases away from him, but still, his voice is in the back, getting more passionate by the minute. I'm laughing, but Nick is less than amused.

* * *

I sit on the couch with my new phone in hand, scrolling through Facebook.

There is so much support from the community and friends. We are all over the news currently. Marco set up a Gofundme page, and so far, we're looking at thirty thousand, but that's barely going to cover all the medical bills. It's impressive, though, the amount of love. It's also upsetting to see the amount of hate. I never really paid attention to homophobes because I never had too. Our situation is even less accepted because not only are we bisexual, but we are committing bigamy, which even gays and lesbians seem to be against.

Katie's giggling interrupts me, and I look up, watching Katie and Nick whisper to each other, making each other smile. She leans over, exposing more of her breasts, and he pulls at the fabric, trying to find a nipple. She pulls back, laughing, "You heard the doctor, as well as I did."

"Doesn't mean we can't play."

"How are you going to last six weeks?"

He snorts, "It will be like a vacation."

Katie scoffs, "Is fucking me work?"

"Yes!"

"You're so old," she bites.

"Not as old as you look."

She turns, pulling her pants down to expose her plump ass, "That is not an old lady ass."

He tries to smack it, but she moves away from him and comes toward me. I toss the phone as her leg swings over me. "Go to sleep, old man." She climbs on my lap, looking over her shoulder at Nick, hoping to make him jealous. "You got something to say?"

"Turn the light on so I can see."

I turn on the light next to me before I grip Katie's ass. "Was that some sort of old couple foreplay?"

Her lips are on mine, and blood rushes to my dick.

With the distance between Nick and me, I feel like I have to love her less, be with her less, to prepare myself for the inevitable. But when she comes to me, I don't have the strength to push her away or hold back. I want all of her just like I want her to want all of me.

I hold her close and put everything to memory. Her vanilla scent. Her soft, smooth skin. The curls of her brown hair. The indent of her throat. The bones of her clavicles. Her fat heavy breasts. The freckle on her hand. The sound of her laugh. The sound of her moans. There's too much I want to remember.

I hold her close as she rides me. All my stresses disappear under her touch, and I have my face pressed between her tits, simply thankful that she's here. Every move is a stab to my rib cage, but I sacrifice pain to be inside her.

"God, Katie, I love you," I murmur against her nipple. She clenches my hair, holding me to her.

"I'm impressed with you," She smiles, her lips by my ear. "You stayed."

I lean back to kiss her parted lips, "I don't want to run anymore. I want to be like you and Nick. Teach me."

She smiles into my mouth, hurrying her pace. "I can be your teacher."

I bit my lip, picturing her in a school uniform with a short skirt. I grip her ass cheeks, moving her faster. The couch squeaks with each bounce. "I'd like it better if you were my student. Then I could spank you when you don't do your homework." I smack her hard and get a beautiful gasp out of her.

Katie pauses, "Hold on." She gets up. My dick is shining with her liquids and I jerk myself. She goes to Nick, kissing him, and attempts to touch his cock, but he shakes his head. "You sure?"

"It's alright. Maybe in a couple of days."

She returns to me, and I gladly help her back on. I can barely move and have to stop myself from trying. She does all the work, and though it takes her longer, I hold off, waiting for the moment I feel her tighten. She struggles to move, so I grip her hips and rock her, bringing her over. With her gripping my cock, I cum inside, digging my nails into her hips. I keep her still so I can empty into her with every desire of impregnating her. I want to give her and Nick a baby more than I want to breathe. And if, by chance, she gets pregnant and I have to go, it will be a 'thank you' gift.

Nine

Tyler: Falling

❧

Finally released, we are driving home. It's been a long-ass week, and even though I'm out of school and I'm not working, I'm exhausted nonetheless. I'm happy Nick's coming home, but at the same time, I don't know what I'm gonna do for space. It's gonna be harder to avoid him with my same excuses. Studying helped me dodge a ton of uncomfortable situations.

As we're pulling onto our street, his lousy attitude returns. There are people outside of our house, and it almost looks like the beginning of a war. They have signs, and I catch one that says 'All Love is Beautiful.' And the opposite says, "Polygamy is illegal!"

"Oh, fuck," I look back at Nick. He's sitting in the back seat with a pillow behind him, shaking his head, his anger brewing with each passing second.

Three reporters are sitting by with their cameras, and as soon as we pull into the driveway, they rush up, spouting questions. "Mr. Mendez, how do you feel about the attack on your life?"

"Mr. Mendez, what are you going to do about the HOA?"

"Mr. Mendez, are you going to lose your job?"

We sit in the car, not knowing what to do.

Nick growls, "This is what talking does. If anything is your fault, it's *this*. Thanks."

I point, "We got a cop, at least."

"I'll get rid of them." Katie whips out of the car, "Get off my property!" she hollers, "Please leave us alone."

They give her space, but they're like mosquitoes, circling, waiting to strike. They still ask their annoying questions over and over again as Katie opens Nick's door. I rush to the other side and help him to his feet. He is walking, but it's slow, more like a shuffle. It's clear his pain pills have worn off because he's panting and sweating by the time we make it to the door. Once we shut it, Snowball attacks, crying and whimpering like she's been alone for a year. I lay Nick on the couch, and he breathes heavily as he pets Snowball, whispering sweet words of love into her face as she licks all his sweat off.

Katie and I turn to the door and look out at the crowds. I hadn't expected this kind of response, and I'm sure Katie hadn't either.

"Why are they talking about the HOA?"

Katie whirls around, "They're just spouting nonsense," she replies with a super tense voice and a forced smile, "You thirsty?" She rushes to the kitchen.

Nick looks at me, and we both know she's lying. He's too tired to fight, but I'm not, and I'm on her heels.

"Katie, what's going on?"

"Nothing."

"You are a terrible liar. What's happening?"

She glares at me as she snatches the water bottle and heads to the couch. "Since you're home, I guess now is a better time than any. The HOA has decided," She pauses, sitting, picking a little fuzzy off the couch to avoid our eyes, "that we should move."

"What?" Nick and I holler.

She holds up her hands to calm us. "They sent us a lengthy letter detailing how we have broken several rules, and they think it would be better if we get out."

Nick rubs his face, and I take a seat staring at the floor. "We can fight this," he decides.

"How?" I wonder blandly.

"Same way I'm fighting my job trying to fire me."

"Fire you?" Katie exclaims. "You own it!"

He ignores her, "Can you get my phone?"

* * *

Everything is falling apart. I feel like my world is crashing. It's the universe telling me to get out before the floor crumbles at my feet. I'm pacing in the bedroom while Katie and Nick are downstairs trying to stall the crash. Don't they ever think that giving up would be easier? It's not a pussy idea some of the time. It's a lifesaver. We can pack our shit and go and start somewhere new. We can run from the assholes that attacked us because if I ever see their face, I'd snatch the knife out of their hands and plow it into their neck.

My fist hits the wall before I realize what I'm doing. The plaster wraps around my knuckles, pieces falling to the floor.

I snap my hand back to my chest, "Ah, fuck." The pain is tremendous, and I stand there just trying to breathe through it. Blood seeps from the scab I made days ago, and I'm hoping the hairline fracture doesn't turn into a full one.

Katie is rushing upstairs, and I turn to her, guilty as fuck, "Sorry." I get out before she can start.

"What happened?"

She figures it out quickly and rushes to the bathroom to grab a rag. She returns to wrap it around my hand, "That's not like you," she murmurs. "What's the matter?"

I can't tell her I'm struggling with staying. I can't tell her I want to kill those fucks that hurt us. I can't tell her that Nick doesn't love me. I can't tell her I'm a fucking pansy for getting my ass beat by a bunch of rednecks. "It was stupid."

She kisses my fingers, "It's okay to be mad, Tyler. You've been through a lot."

"I'm fine."

"No, you're not. I hope you talk to me before I'm driving around town looking for you."

"I'm not going anywhere."

"Promise me something."

"Like what?"

"If you can't talk to me, find someone to talk to."

I step out of her arms, moving out of the room, "I told you I'm fine, just drop it."

Ten

Tyler: Rough

Two weeks since Nick's blood drenched my hands. I've always wanted to become a surgeon, diving into body parts, fixing what's broken. Having blood on my hands never bothered me. It's Nick's blood, however, that keeps me awake at night. I think of all the things I should have done differently. I should have fought harder. Instead of being on the defense and just protecting myself from the onslaught, I should have been on the attack, like Nick had been. He fought like a fucking gladiator while I fought like a bitch. If I hadn't let that last guy go, if I had managed to break his foot as I intended, Nick would have been safe.

I stare at the ceiling, watching the fight unfold in the dark. Anger is a stunted emotion compared to what I feel. I want to break their legs. I want to make them suffer. I want them to know fear like I did when I saw that knife go into Nick's back.

Katie's hand slips under my shirt. I look over at her, and she's awake with a mischievous smile. Her hand dips into my boxers and grips my sleeping cock. I almost want to tell her, no, but I don't want her to think anything is wrong. I don't know if I can even get it up, but I'll let her try. She slinks downward till her mouth wraps up my penis. She can take the whole thing in when it isn't hard, and her lips press against my pelvis, and she hums. I close my eyes, allowing the pleasure to overtake my rage. She works me with diligence, doing all her tongue tricks.

"You're distracted tonight."

"Keep going, I'll get there."

It takes an extra-long time to get me hard enough, but she never wavers, and as soon as I'm fully erect, she sits on me, burying my cock deep into her pussy. I watch her breasts flop with each hard bounce.

Nick shifts from the noise, looking over at us, "It's 2 in the morning," he mumbles.

Katie leans over and reaches under the blanket, but he once again bats her away.

"I'm sleeping," he rolls on his side, "Be quiet."

I bring her attention back to me, latching onto her hips so I can fuck her from the bottom. She leans over me, her big breasts hitting me in the face and her breath in my ear as she tries to suppress her moans. I smack her on the ass in retaliation. I'm not going to be quiet for his lazy ass. I'm fucking my fiancee with all the effort she deserves.

This is what I should be focusing on: Her pussy. It melts my temper and relaxes me. I drown in her.

I let her take over, the pain in my ribs derailing my efforts. Her hips rotate back and forth as she keeps me deep inside her. I reach over to the dresser, grab a small finger vibrator, and press it up against her clit. Her moans get louder, and her movement is more focused.

Nick suddenly gets up, grabbing his pillow, and stalks out. Katie and I humorously meet each other's eyes, but our attention remains on our movements. She doesn't even attempt to go after him with the vibrator making her convulse.

I pull away before she can cum and toss her off, if only to get up on my knees. I grab her ankles, spreading her legs in a 'v', fucking her slow.

"Let's go downstairs," she pants. "I want him to be able to sleep, and he hates the couch."

I take my time with the request, waiting until we are both near the edge before I pull out. She curses at me, and I smack her ass on the way down.

Katie leans over Nick, kissing him, "Baby, go upstairs; we'll stay down here."

He reaches up and grabs her boob. "I'm up now."

She giggles and kisses him.

I interrupt, sticking into her from behind. She gasps into his mouth and looks over her shoulder. Her breasts now swing in front of his face, and he sticks his tongue out to tease a nipple.

I change up my position when I'm close to cumming. Six, seven times, and Katie simply follows my moves, obeying blindly. Once more, I have her bent over the couch, and with every hard thrust, she pants a little moan. Katie grips the pillows, her face buried into one. She's getting tired, but I don't care. Over an hour of fucking, and I'm panting, sweating, refusing to stop. I'd much rather be doing this than thinking.

I put a leg up on the armrest, getting in deep, making her moans turn into wild pleasurable cries. Our bodies collide with a smack over and over like clapping hands.

"Too deep," she gasps.

"Take it," I order. My hands grip her hips, forcing her to meet me.

A hand presses against me, and she surrenders, "Break."

I pull out of her, giving in to her request reluctantly.

I want more.

I want it harder.

Her pussy juice drips from me, getting on the floor. I take off my shirt and clean my legs and cock with it. "Go lay down."

She stumbles over to Nick, wobbling and weak. She lays down with her legs spread, her pussy open to the room. With her head on Nick's lap, she puts his cock in her mouth, and it pokes at her cheek. I grab her legs and fold her over like a blanket, so her ass is in the air. Nick grabs her ankles, keeping them nearly to her head. I pack on the lube before I'm pushing my dick into her asshole. It no longer bends or meets resistance. She's been well-prepped to take it hard. I shove in, and Nick's dick pops out of her mouth as she curses.

I wrap my hand around her throat, choking her the way she enjoys it. I bite her leg, leaving imprints on her skin. She barely feels it while I'm deep in her ass.

Nick's hand grips my hair momentarily, and I can feel the slight push, silent in his request to suck his cock. I lean back on my knees, putting space between us. He meets my eye for a slight second before he brings his attention back to Katie, slapping his tip against her open lips.

I smack the back of Katie's thighs, loving the sound it makes.

"Baby, I can't take anymore," she pants, "Please, cum."

I lick my fingers and rub them over her clit. She bucks and twists, but I keep her steady, rubbing her pussy lips like a disc jockey.

"Cum. Grip my cock."

I stop pounding, if only to concentrate on her clit. I spit on it and then scrub it like the damn rug. Her mouth is open, completely forgetting about Nick, and she can only cry. She grips my wrist, trying to stop me, but I bring her over the edge, and her body convulses, her asshole gripping me like a vice. "Oh god!" She cries out, a deep guttural sound that comes from her gut. Despite how easy she is to get off, I'm still proud when I give her a 'level 10' orgasm, as she claims.

Guys only have three levels: Good, great, and fucking amazing. But obviously, women are much more complicated than that. A level 10 is the hardest to get, but I always know when she makes it because of her cry. Every time we fuck, I aim for that, but it usually takes a long time. I've also been trying to figure out ways to make her squirt, but if she hasn't done it by now, I don't know if she can. I've done some pretty intense shit to her pussy.

I resume pounding into her ass, and shortly, I cum deep inside her. The release is long-awaited, and my legs shake from the stress. "Don't move," I slowly pull out of her, and Nick keeps hold of her ankles while I grab a phone off the counter, and with a bright light on, I record as my cum slowly trickles out of her anus. It's a beautiful fucking sight.

"I hate it when you do that. It's gross."

I throw a shirt at her, "I see a lot of gross stuff. Believe me, baby, it's fucking hot."

"Hey," Nick barks, holding his hard-on. "What about me?"

I keep walking, "I'm gonna go shower."

I'm pissed again. It didn't take that long to be overwhelmed with anger, but Nick's audacity set me off. He wants me to blow him after telling me he needs time. If I've ever felt more

62

like an escort, it's now. He doesn't give a shit about me. He just wants his cock sucked.

I'm in the shower when Katie pops in. She is still naked and slips in with me, wrapping her arms around me. The muscles in my jaw release, and I sigh out, sinking into her under the water. I almost want to apologize for overreacting, as if she can hear the rampant thoughts in my head.

I want to fuck again. When I focus on her, I can breathe. I kiss her neck, moving down to her breast,

"Sweetie, I'm hurting. Look at me."

I rest my forehead on hers, sighing.

"What's going on with you and Nick?"

"Nothing."

She pulls back and looks at me, "I'm not blind. You haven't touched him since we got home from the hospital."

I shrug, "We had a disagreement."

"That's what he said."

"I'm not shooting my mouth off anymore. If Nick wants to talk, it's up to him."

"I'm part of this too, so tell me what's going on."

I rub the soap out of my hair, ignoring her. Nick and I haven't talked to her about us. She never knew we were going to get married. She didn't know I was falling in love with him. I could never say the words aloud. I was waiting for Nick to be ready. Now I know he never will be.

If I tell her everything now, she's gonna tell me that I'm asking for too much, just like Nick. That's one of the bad things about being in a 'Throuple'. There are sides.

"Can we go out tomorrow? Me and you? I need to get out of the house."

She forces a smile, "Sure."

Eleven

Tyler: Break

⁂

Before Katie and I leave for our date, I tell her I'm not going to talk about Nick, and thankfully she accepts it. We go hiking in the Poconos, visiting waterfalls, and hanging out over cliffs. It makes me realize how long it's been since I've taken the time to enjoy the outdoors. School took so much from me, but hopefully, it will all be worth it. As I sit on a rock, overlooking the great expense of the woods with Katie sitting between my legs, I finally feel like myself again. I'm relaxed and clear-headed.

"Are you feeling better?"

I nod into her hair.

"You haven't been sleeping."

I don't respond, unable to come up with any reasonable excuse.

"You've been crappy. Almost mean sometimes. You are

always at the gym. I'm really worried."

Though she believes all I do is go to the gym, I'm actually going to appointments for my heart. In the last week, I've gone every day for a few hours getting a full workup, trying to gauge the damage and the level of heart failure. I'm thankful she hasn't noticed any of the needle pricks in my arms.

"Just stress." Which is true. I've never dealt with so much stress all at once. I'm surprised I'm managing.

"Can I help at all?"

I kiss her temple, "You already are. Just breathing you relaxes me." I take a deep breath in her ear, and she giggles, making me smile. "You know what really relaxes me?"

She groans, "You're gonna kill me."

Sarcastically, I reply, "Oh, is it too much for you?"

"It's never enough."

"That's what I thought."

"My pussy kind of hurts, though."

"Take some Tylenol."

She looks at me, scratching my face. "Are you…" she pauses. "What?"

"I don't want to say it because I don't want to make you mad."

"I'm not that bad."

"Sometimes, you are. I am just wondering if you're using sex to escape."

With annoyance, I pull away from her, but she grips onto me, "We started this relationship fucking, and then you're shocked when I want to fuck?"

"No. NO, that's not it at all."

"Then what's different? We have sex all the time, but yet now, I have an agenda?"

"It's different."

"Why?"

"Because you're rougher."

"You like it rough. This conversation is bullshit; you know that, right? You're reminding me of my bitchy ex-girlfriend."

"Hey."

I grit my teeth, looking away.

"Tyler. Look at me."

I force myself to meet her gaze.

"I love you," she touches my face, and my eyes close. The sudden rage is smothered, and I hang my head. She hugs me. "Want me to suck your cock behind that tree?"

I laugh, hugging her. It takes me a minute but eventually, I give in, "I'm sorry, baby. There's stuff I'm dealing with on my own. And yeah, fucking you helps. But you said I'm rough. Did I hurt you?"

"Just a little yesterday."

"I'll make it up to you."

She looks at me with a devilish grin. "How?"

Back home, I'm once again taking her clothes off as we climb the stairs. Everything else may be fucked up right now but being inside her is the only normal thing.

My dick is pressing through my jeans, and each chance I get, I rub against her. Her shirt is gone by the front door. Her pants are at the bottom of the stairs. I leave her in her panties and bra; her beautiful fit body is better than porn stars.

We drop in bed with Nick sleeping next to us. I'm between her legs, pulling her panties to the side and digging into a delicious fucking meal of pussy. Her hands are in my hair, keeping my face pushed against her juicy lips. She leans over Nick, waking him up by rubbing his flaccid dick and pulling at his balls. I don't want her paying any attention to him. I want all of her focus.

I pull her lips apart and find her clit, rolling my tongue against it over and over again. She falls back on the bed, arching her back, surrendering to the pleasure. She is so easy; she nearly cums already, but I back out and bite her thigh, calming her down. She pants, her breasts heaving with every inhale.

"Katie, sit on my face," Nick interrupts.

She shifts to move to him, but I grip her, "I'm not done."

"Get your cocked sucked. I want her pussy." Nick pulls on her arm, "Come on."

I grip her leg, "I'm busy."

"Katie."

"Katie."

Katie gets up and stands in front of the bed, "This isn't working. What's going on with you two?"

I sit back on my heels, "Wait your goddamn turn."

"Excuse me? This is my wife."

"No, asshole, she is ours."

"Stop!" Katie yells at us. "This isn't about me. What the hell happened with you guys?"

Nick rolls his eyes, "He's just pissed I'm not as gay as him."

I hop off the bed, enraged and yet finding this funny as hell. "You realize you were just stabbed for being gay, so maybe have a talk with your God about that fuck up." I look to Katie, "You want to know what happened? I told this fucker I loved him, and he told me I'm convenient so here we are," I walk to the door, "I'm going downstairs."

"Good, run away."

I squeeze my fist, stalling in the doorway to glare back at him. Then I decide it's not worth it and keep moving.

* * *

I'm sitting outside with Snowball's head in my lap. It's one of those times I wish I smoked. I need something to relax me, and if I can't fuck might as well smoke. But instead, I pet the dog. She looks at me with her brown eyes, and it forces a smile. I rest my forehead down on hers.

The sliding glass opens, and Katie walks out. I sit back silent, and Snowball slinks back inside. I've been out here for nearly an hour. I'm sure Katie and Nick talked, but I don't want to talk about it.

"How come you didn't tell me that you are in love with Nick?"

I shrug. "It's just something that I'm dealing with."

"We're supposed to talk to each other."

"I didn't want you to get all happy, and then it not work out. Like it's not. Like I knew it wouldn't."

"I could have helped."

"How?"

"I know Nick better than you," she sits down beside me, "It's you I can't figure out sometimes."

"Really? I feel like an open book."

She giggles, "You do have a lot to say. But nothing about how you feel. I know you've had trouble talking about things in the past. But this is a big deal. This could destroy us."

Katie sighs, staring at the woods. We have a deer family that pokes their heads out from time to time, but it's too late at night for them. "Nick is making progress. Can you wait for a little more?"

I knew she would take his side. It pisses me off. "That's all I've been giving him, is time."

"Would Nick be with you and not have feelings for you? Do you think he's that type of guy? So he's not shouting to the world that he loves you. I'm pretty sure he can't even admit it to himself. But look at everything he's done. He has to think pretty highly of you to be okay with us getting married. To be in this relationship."

"I know. I know," I stand moving to the end of the deck.

"Then what do you want? I mean, he agreed to marry you," she laughs, so amazed by the idea. "Why would he do that?"

"He told me it was convenient."

"He said he didn't mean that."

"He told me straight up he would never love me."

"I'm sure he didn't mean that either."

"How do I know that? How do you? We keep getting deeper into this, and I'm not even sure he wants it."

"Of course he does—"

"He could be doing all of this for you. Doesn't that bother you?"

"But he's not."

"How do you know?"

She struggles with a response, "I just do."

"Well, I'm not that intuitive, I guess."

"I just don't think you're ever going to get a flat-out answer, Tyler. Why do you need it?"

I didn't think I would need a reason. Wouldn't anyone want an answer? "Nick could have died. I failed to protect him."

Katie is unprepared with that response, and it takes her a moment to get up and come to me. She rests her head on my arm, "Baby, you couldn't have done anything."

"I let him go. The guy with the knife. I let him go."

"You didn't know what those men were capable of. You saved

Nick."

I shove away from her, "I didn't save him! I put him in that position. It's my fault he was stabbed. It's why I need to know if this is what he wants. I can't stay and risk him or you if he doesn't want me here. It's not worth it."

"He's told you he wants you to stay."

"For you! All he's ever done is for you."

She stands there looking broken. Tears are in her eyes, and for a moment, neither one of us know what to say. She knows I'm right. She knows Nick has gone above and beyond for her own happiness, but if he isn't in this for himself, then how can we keep doing what we're doing?

"And what about me?" she wonders in a whisper, "You're gonna leave me if he doesn't love you?"

My brows knit in sadness, "How can I stay?"

"You'll break my heart."

I reach for her, taking her cheeks into my hands, "I don't want too, baby, but what should I do? Tell me, and I'll do anything you say."

"I don't know," she whimpers, water dripping over my thumbs. "What do *I* do? How am I supposed to choose between you and him? I can't. I couldn't."

I rest my forehead on hers, "I wouldn't ask you to choose, Katie."

She closes her eyes as the tears pour out of them. She grabs my shirt, squeezing the fabric in a tight fist. "Please. Please, just a little more time? Give me and him more time."

I hold her. I hold her like there will be a time when I can't anymore.

Twelve

Tyler: Advice

I exit another bar, infuriated. I can't find that fucker. I kick a trash can, and it flies before it bounces into the street. The homeless guy against the wall curses at me, but I stuff my hands in my pockets and keep moving.

It's like he just disappeared. No one's heard of the guy that stabbed Nick. No one knows a thing. It's bullshit. They're liars. They are all goddamn liars. Just a bunch of hicks and hillbillies sticking up for each other.

I get to my car and drive. I should get home. Katie will start texting me soon. But home isn't exactly a fun place. I moved into my office simply so I don't have to deal with Nick. Katie's been miserable, which is exactly the reason why I kept her out of my business. She always has to be involved. She stopped planning the wedding, and now it's like a funeral parlor in our home.

The only good thing is, she still comes to me. Every night, she comes in, and instead of fucking, I make sure she knows that my feelings for her haven't changed any. Our lovemaking is slow and passionate and done with every ounce of desire I possess. She's the only reason I go home at night.

Otherwise, I'd stay out and find those douche bags that fucked with us. I got my own knife now. We'll see who wins next time.

They caught one more guy but not the man that stabbed Nick. It should feel like a victory, but it's not. Our lawyer is telling us to drop charges in the fear of AFA retaliation. The same lawyer told us we have no case against the HOA. The same lawyer told us Nick can't win against Arthur about his company.

Against better judgment, I've asked my father to help. I don't know what he can do, but maybe he'll have some ideas. And if nothing else, being in his presence might stop my free fall.

I meet him at a restaurant. Every time I see him, I feel like he's getting older. It's not fair. I want him in my life, but how can I? He's made it clear he doesn't accept me or my three-way relationship. I've told David (Nick and Katie don't know I'm here) just in case my father hired someone to kidnap me and take me off to a rehab facility. As silly as that sounds, he's done it before.

I stand as he approaches, and he forces a stiff smile. He holds out his hand, and I grip it, "How was your flight?"

"You're almost healed?"

"Almost," I lift my shirt to show the fading yellow skin, the bruises on my ribs the only lasting discoloration. I have a scar on my eyebrow, but it's white and barely noticeable.

He nods and sits. The server comes right up to us. He orders a drink and a sandwich. I don't order and he takes it upon himself, "You need to eat. Get him a salad with fruit" He hands the menus back. "How's your heart? You take your medications every day?"

"Yes. I said I would."

Sensing my aggravation, he brings up the reason he's here, "So you said you wanted to talk about your attack. Did they catch the people that did this?"

"Two of the three. Nick and I had to go down and identify them. But the problem is getting a lawyer."

"They should appoint you one."

"We have one, but they're advising us to drop it."

"Do you have the man that stabbed your friend?"

"No."

"You have the proof. The security footage? Concentrate on him. He's the only one you'll be able to convict."

I knew this, and the fact that I'm still unable to catch him rattles me to the core. My fists clench against my thighs, "I feel like we are getting attacked from all sides. Our HOA is kicking us out. Nick's job is trying to steal his company. I don't know what to do."

"This is what you chose-"

"Alright," I get up.

He grabs my arm, "Stop, stop, stop. Don't be dramatic, sit down."

It would be really funny to tell him Nick says that to me all the time but I don't think it would help me. It's also a punch to the gut because I never saw myself as 'dramatic'.

Samuel takes a drink, glancing around, taking a breather. "You want honest advice, unbiased. I can do that. But you aren't going to like what I have to say."

"That's fine. I can stand it when it's helpful."

"Polyandry, where a woman has more than one lover, is

illegal, not just partial or in some areas like polygamy but in every country of the world. So whatever the HOA has, or the job is saying, you can't legally fight it. They can push back, get you, your girlfriend-"

"Fiancee,"

"You'll get thrown in jail. That's the law—two to six years imprisonment for bigamy. If you want to get away with it, it's better to just stay under the radar. No one will have a problem with it until you start reaching for things like the gay community. Like healthcare or marriage."

"So don't want typical life needs."

"Are you trying to become an advocate for bigamy?"

"No."

"Then stay your lane. You want to do what you do and not bother anyone. It's taken the gay community decades to get where they are at, and they are still fighting for equal rights," he snaps his fingers, "I got it."

"Got what?"

"Get yourself an LGBT lawyer."

"I'm not gay."

He pauses, "I thought you and your friend are, you know."

"Yeah, so?"

"Use that. Keep the girl out of it."

"Nick and Katie, dad. Use their names."

"You want to fight me or the HOA? You pose gay, correct all these reports about polyandry, say it was a mistake or misunderstood. They'll get off your case. No one wants to deal with the gay activists."

"And Katie? What's she?"

"Roommate?"

"They're married."

He stops to think, chewing on a french fry. "I got a guy that could help. Owes me. Dropped a case against his sister. Stealing underwear." He chuckles, pulling out his glasses, slipping them on then takes out his phone. He still holds it far from his face trying to see the little numbers. I love it and hate it. It's just like him but an older him. It points out how much I've missed him.

"I don't get you, dad."

"What?"

"Why are you helping?"

He sets the phone down, taking a drink, "When you have a kid, you'll get it. I hate what you are doing, Adam. I hate it. I don't support it. I want the best for you, and this isn't it. I can't stand it sometimes when I think about it. I want you to join a program." He reaches into his pocket and takes out a brochure. "Your name is already on the list."

I take the paper, unsurprised.

"But I love you, and I'll always be here when you need help."

I bite the inside of my cheek. I'm starting to wonder if I'm more emotional than I want to be. "I miss you. I miss mom."

"She always knew you were bound for something. Ray, not so much."

I laugh, and he chuckles.

"I knew it too, which is why I'm struggling with your choices. But you did make it through medical school. I guess some good came out of it."

"They're really great people, dad."

"I don't care. They can be freaking Gandhi. They are leading you down a bad path. You think being jumped is normal? It's a sign, Adam. You don't need them. I would have paid for medical school."

"But you didn't."

"You quit to be a hooker. If you needed more money, all you had to do was ask."

"I was nineteen, in college, being paid to have sex with girls. What more do I need to say to make you understand? It didn't matter how much money you gave me." It's supposed to be a joke, but he doesn't find it funny.

"It's supposed to be an act for two people in love—"

I roll my eyes, "You're so old school. No one does that anymore."

"What if you had a child—"

"I was always careful."

"Or an STD?"

"Well, that happens, but nothing I couldn't fix."

He puts his hands to his ear, "No more."

I chuckle. I pick at my food to find a different topic.

"You've lost weight. And you look like crap. Why?"

I shrug. My depression is like a boulder on my shoulders, and the moment he acts as if he cares, it weakens my walls. I blink rapidly, hating the fact there are actually tears in my eyes. I feel like a little kid that just wants to bury themselves into their parents' lap. It's an urge that's hard to fight.

"I don't know if you'll have to worry about Nick and Katie soon."

"Why?"

I shrug again. I know my dad doesn't care, but I want him too. "We're fighting."

"People fight. Your mother and I fought all the time. She was a democrat."

I smile, rolling my eyes.

"You know," Samuel sits back, folding his arms, "I was waiting for this."

"For what?"

"For you to give up."

"What's that mean?"

"I think the reason you don't give up on school is because of your mother. She made you love learning. You asked for a series of encyclopedias for your tenth birthday." He pauses, taking a drink. I wait impatiently, wondering what his point is.

I know I'm not much of a fighter, but for him to expect it, really gets on my nerves.

"But you gave up every sport you ever started. You gave up every friendship you ever had. I don't even think you ever had a best friend. Except for Ray, but he doesn't count. Maybe it was the homeschooling that made you so closed off. Or maybe it was me. But whatever it was, I knew I only had to wait."

"Why are you saying this?"

"Just making an observation," he taps on the paper, "When you're ready." Samuel gets up, "I'll be in town for one more day." He lays money on the table and walks out.

Thirteen

Tyler: Care

~·~

As I pull up to the house, Nick's dad's car sits in my spot, so I pull up on the side of the road. I like Nick's dad, but I go to lengths to avoid him. He's become a priest in the last year and wants to talk about the fictitious God. Otherwise, he's a real down-to-earth type of guy. Easy to get along with just like Nick.

I'm on my way up the front steps when the door opens.

"Descansa y hablamos luego, hijo."

"Esta bien."

I hold the door open for him, and Joseph greets me with a smile. His hair is gray, and he has wrinkles all over him. His belly proceeds him, but despite it, he's aging well. "Tyler, how are you?"

"I'm good, sir; how are you?"

"Walk me to my car."

He slaps a hand on my back and looks over my face. "Any more pain?"

I shake my head, "I'm better. Just waiting for the bruises to fade." Joseph touches my head, the fresh white scar on my brow, and then pats me on the back of the neck.

"Good."

I watch his feet as he goes down the stairs, fearing he'll fall. I keep my hands out, waiting to catch him, but he chuckles and swats at me, "I'm not senile. So what's been going on, son?"

"What do you mean?"

"Katie called me last night and said you hadn't been yourself since the attack."

I blow out air and shake my head. Sometimes Katie needs to mind her own business. She tries to fix everything, and though I love that about her, it's also annoying.

"As a priest, many people come to me for advice. If you ever need someone to talk too, I hope you feel comfortable with me."

"I'm good," I reply a bit harshly. I try again, "Thank you, but I'm okay."

"It's okay to be angry, Tyler. It wasn't fair what happened. Believe me; I have had my moments, moments I'm not proud of. His mother…" he chuckles, "said some words I didn't know she knew. But be assured that you will have your vengeance."

I look at him surprised, but Joseph smiles, "God will avenge you. Leave it in His hands. Let this anger go and know that it is already taken care of."

Out of respect, I don't reply, but I struggle to suppress the aggravation. I open his door for him, but he stands in front of me with no intention of getting in.

"What happened was not your fault. I hope you know that."

I shake my head, bite my cheek and say nothing.

"Perhaps it was my fault," Joseph admits, bowing his head.

"Why would it be your fault?"

"I asked God to show me a sign. To help me accept this relationship. To help me accept you. And He did. You saved my son's life."

"I put him in danger. If I drank and drove and crashed and nearly killed him, would I still be a hero?"

"You think you had any control over those men?"

"I talk too much."

"You are taking the blame for intolerance. Tell me, at what point is it their fault? You did not go out and pick a fight. You did not throw the first punch. None of this is your fault. Here I thought you were angry at them. But you are angry at yourself."

I drop my head, toeing the grass, avoiding, wondering if it would be rude just to walk away.

"Nicholas feels the same way. He knew about the AFA and ignored them. But even that is not his fault. The control lies with those men. They did what they did to be malicious. To be hateful. They are to blame. And they will be held accountable. But not by you. Vengeance will only damage you further." He puts a hand on my shoulder, "Let me bear your burden. All your anger lay it on me. I will hold it for you." Joseph pulls me in and hugs me, something my own father failed to do. "I am very proud of you, and I am happy you are in my son's life."

I clench my eyes shut, unwilling to give in, to cling to him the way I want too. I tap his arm, showing my appreciation, and he let's go, smiling, slapping my arm once more before he gets into his car.

I stand there for a long time, wishing my own father showed the same compassion. Somehow, he knew exactly what I needed to hear. But I don't know how to give him my anger. I don't know how to let go. Or perhaps I don't want to. I want to be angry at them because Nick deserves revenge.

Inside, Nick is on the phone and waves absentmindedly. I sit on the couch and start up a video game, hoping to drown out everything up till this point.

Nick has the phone on speaker, and it's impossible to ignore.

"I'm not doing this to hurt you, Nick. This is for the business."

"It's my business."

"You keep saying that, and I keep reminding you, it's our business. Fifty, Fifty. I'm willing to buy you out. Just take the money, man."

"I love my job. I'm good at it. I run that restaurant in my fucking sleep."

"I can't risk it any more than we already have. You promised that your life wouldn't jeopardize the restaurant. Now we have protesters at our door saying we're going to Hell and a bunch of LGBT people dressing up as fucking drag queens telling them that all love is equal. Our clientele has dropped significantly. We are down over forty percent this week. Our customers don't want to deal with your shit, and neither do I."

"I know. I know," Nick sighs, tapping on the counter. I hate how easy he gives in.

"I'm asking you to do what's best for our business before you sink it."

"How can I walk away? All the hours. All the promises."

"If Katie wants that kind of life, then she's gonna have to accept the consequences. Just like you do."

I toss the controller, jumping to my feet, "Give me the phone."

"Arthur, I'll call you back."

As I reach for it, he hangs up and glares at me. "Don't help.

God knows what you'll do."

"'Face the consequences.' Fuck him."

"I know it may seem like a shock to you, but there *are* consequences to our actions."

"Spare me the lecture."

"Tyler."

I swing around, "What?"

"Let's go to the shooting range."

All my fight deflates, and I think about it. I have never shot a gun before. Nick goes every other week with his brother, but I haven't been invited. In his defense, I never wanted to go. My thoughts of a shooting range are a bunch of rednecks and white supremacists gathered around talking about how great being white is.

"Martin can't?"

"Martin's gonna meet us there. He says there's a surprise, but I already know about his new truck."

"He knows I'm coming?"

"No. But it's not going to be a problem."

Shooting a gun is what I need right now. "Alright."

Fourteen

Tyler: Shooting Range

W e don't talk on the way there. I stare at the window, and the radio plays his Spanish music. I'm fine with it. I'm still thinking about Joseph's words and how to go about handing him my anger. Anger isn't physical, so just tossing it away doesn't sound rational.

The parking lot is full, and Nick announces, "We have a big group that joins us. About twenty. Friends I've had since college. They can be a little much so ignore it."

On our way in, a group of four spots him, and they holler. The only black guy in the group rushes over, "Nick! Back from the dead." They slap hands, a quick hug, "Looking good with one less kidney."

Nick laughs and slaps his belly, "I recommend it. Lost ten pounds already. Guys, this is Tyler."

I expect the inevitable, the pause, the awkward silence, but instead, it's, "The guy that saved you? Oh, Shit." Wyatt holds out his hand, and I slap it. He hugs me quickly, too, "You did the world a favor; this guy is too good to lose." One by one, they all greet me, and it's welcoming, but it's probably because they don't know who I am really. I'm not Nick's boyfriend. I'm 'the guy that saved him.'

A whistle sounds, "Hey, you faggots, let's go." It's Martin at the door.

When the group grumbles, I feel like I'm with my own people, and my anxiety falls away. "Don't know how you and him are brothers."

I chime in, "I wonder about that every damn day."

When Martin sees me, his smile fades. He pulls Nick off to the side, but he isn't quiet about it, "Why'd you bring him?"

Nick slaps him on the shoulder, "Remember what we talked about?"

Martin rolls his eyes before he forces out an agitated, "Hey."

Guess we're back to the whole 'nice' routine, "Hey."

Inside, Nick is just as surprised as me with the decorations and banner saying, 'Welcome back!' and Martin grins, "I did this," he announces proudly.

"We all did it," Wyatt adds.

Nick dives into the crowd, all waiting to say hello. It's a bunch of older white men with a sprinkle of women and black people. It's not far from what I thought a shooting range would look like in the middle of Pennsylvania. I'm surprised they haven't excommunicated him, considering they should all know he's in a poly-ship by now.

I follow Nick, interested in his life here. He never talks about the shooting range, simply because Katie hates it. He has so many friends, and they seem to accept him.

Nick brings us up to the front desk. Against the wall are dozens of guns, all different shapes, and sizes. It's intimidating. I've never seen so many weapons before. "Nick!" The man behind it greets.

"Rory, what's up, bro?"

"Should you be out?"

"It's been a couple of weeks. I can stand at least."

"You should be used to being stabbed by now."

Wide-eyed, I turn to Nick, but he's laughing, "Fuck you. By the way, this is Tyler."

"Speaking of getting stabbed, *The* Tyler?"

Nick laughs, shaking his head, "The only."

"Wow, good to meet you, bro. Better looking and younger. Sure this isn't a midlife crisis?"

"I'm not mid-way yet."

"With the way you eat, you sure are. So what are you shooting today? You gonna do the shotgun? Get some aggression out?"

"No, I need something with a little less power."

"I got ya. What about you? What are you shooting?"

I stand like a fish, but Nick answers for me, "He needs the shotgun."

"Fuck ya, he does. They get the guys that attacked you yet?"

"Two of them. The third one's out there somewhere."

Rory puts a gun in front of Nick and leans over, "So don't look but in the right corner by the snack machine. They got a tattoo, a swastika. You stay away from them, alright?"

It's instant how I swing toward them. I search their faces, hoping to see anything that looks familiar. If that guy is here, could I stop myself from attacking? I have my knife on me, I could stab them without them even knowing what the hell's going on. Does it even matter if it isn't them? He represents the whole fucked up organization.

Nick slaps me on the shoulder to bring my attention back to them, "I'm less afraid than I have ever been."

"You cocky ass. How do you handle it, Tyler, his ego?"

"I've seen his dick."

Rory busts out, cackling, "Oh shit!"

Nick attacks, playfully punching and slapping me, and I'm laughing, scampering away. It's the first time we've just messed with each other in a long time, and it feels good. It's always been easy slipping into the friend zone with Nick. He's funny, and he takes just as much as he gives. He's comfortable here, and when he's comfortable, it sinks into me, and I can be myself.

"He's kidding. He was limping for days."

Once again, he shocks me. He's so open with our situation here. I don't get it. Why is he a big prude at work?

Rory snickers as he rests the guns in front of us with the ammo on the side. "Teach him the rules, Nick."

"I got it."

Martin is never too far, and as we walk up, he approaches, "Can you keep the flirting to a minimum at least?"

Nick doesn't even stop, "Everyone knows, Martin. You made sure of that."

"You still holding that against me?"

"What?" I ask.

"About five months ago, Martin got drunk and told everyone that his little brother was fucking a guy. What he didn't expect was everyone not to give a shit."

"I said I was sorry."

Nick meets my eye, "So you think the AFA found out from you, but I think the AFA found out from him. What are the chances of a member of a hate group coming into my fancy restaurant? Then what are the chances they come to a gun range?"

"Can we just shoot?" Martin stalks away.

Nick smiles, "He's a little sore about it."

"So they all know who I am?"

"Yeah."

"And you're okay with that?"

"It sucked in the beginning. It's all they wanted to talk about. Two of the guys that hung with us since college kind of left because of it. They think because I've been with a guy that anytime I look at them, I'm hitting on them. But whatever. It's better now. They don't care anymore. Alright, let me teach you the rules."

Fifteen

Tyler: Dense

⟡

Shooting a shotgun changes my life.

It gives me back my sense of control. I feel powerful like my manhood is restored. The power beneath my fingertips is what it feels like to make Katie cum. It's the same kind of release, and when all the bullets are spent, I just stand there, relieved of all my stress, staring at the great big hole in my target.

I leave the room and remove my earplugs, showing my work to Nick. He's sitting at the table with a smile, "How'd you like it?"

I sit with him, "Almost better than sex."

He nods, "Exactly. Katie doesn't get it."

"She ever come?"

"The first year. She can shoot pretty good, but she says it stresses her. I don't know how but whatever." He eases back, holding his side.

I observe him, noticing the slight change in his presence. He is a little pale and looks tired, "You bring any pain pills?"

"Yeah, I just took some."

"This was a lot to do the first time out. Let's get back."

Nick shakes his head, looking around, "Like it better than sitting in front of the TV."

We sit, watching people shoot through the Plexiglas. Every once in and awhile, someone will come up to him. They talk about his recovery, about the men that beat us up. Every time he makes sure to tell them how I saved his life. I'm not angry about it anymore. I'm depressed because I wish I had. I wish I had put up a decent fight as he did for me.

Nick leans up on the table after the last person walks away and looks at me. I feel his eyes and meet his gaze. "What?"

"Do you feel better? You've been angry and moody as hell these past few weeks. And I know I'm part of the reason, but getting jumped didn't help."

"I'm alright."

He drops a hand under the table and rests it on my knee. I glance around, making sure no one is looking for his sake. "Katie told me you think you have to leave."

"I don't see another choice."

"I told you I don't want you to go."

I move my knee away, "You don't want to talk here."

"Yeah, I do.

I clench my teeth, looking at him, "I don't want to go, but I'm not going to force you into a relationship because of me and Katie."

"You're not."

"How can I believe you? You'd do anything for Katie. You're

89

letting another man have a baby with her because you can't—"

"I'm letting *you* have a baby with her. Ty, why don't you see it?"

"It's all for Katie, Nick."

"No—" He cuts himself off, being too loud, glancing around. He lowers his voice, "It's not."

"The only reason I'm here is because Katie wanted a three-some. The only reason I stayed is because Katie wanted me to stay. The only reason we kissed is because Katie wanted us to. Our whole relationship is based on what Katie wants. I can't tell the difference between your wants and her wants. Can you? Can you honestly sit here and tell me that you, you alone, want me to stay?"

Nick sits there, staring at the table with his arms folded. He almost looks angry, but what has he to be upset about? I'm the one that's 'convenient. He said he didn't mean it, but it came from somewhere. He took it back because he didn't want to be a dick, but it had to be the truth.

His brows knit, and he shakes his head, looking away.

"What?"

"Give me a minute. I don't want to yell."

"Oh, you're pissed? Screw you. I'm the one you're fucking using," I move to go.

"Sit down. I said give me a goddamn minute."

I fall back in the chair roughly, glaring now at our surroundings. This wasn't a good place to do this. I don't get why he thought we should talk about us here. I just want to go home.

"So tell me if I got this right. You think I brought up the thought of having a baby with Katie, for Katie only. You think I agreed to accept your gay-ass proposal, the one she didn't know about, for Katie. You think I took a stab to the back for

Katie. You think I brought you here, introduced you to all of my friends that I had for years, for Katie. You think I'm facing losing my company, my house, losing my goddamn Soul, nearly losing my life for Katie. And now you're suggesting I'm only using you to what? To fuck? Because fucking a guy was on my bucket list? Jeezes Tyler, if you're this dense, I don't know what to tell you."

"You—"

He stops me with a quick hand and greets Wyatt as the guy walks up to us. "We're all going out for a drink; you guys want to come?"

The more seconds that pass, the more confused I get. Have I been ignoring all of it? He had told me himself he didn't love me, that he would never love me, but maybe Katie's right. He can't even admit it to himself, so how could I ever expect him to reveal it to me? His actions have far exceeded love. What if some of the things he's done have actually been for me? I never thought about that before.

"No, we're gonna go home. I'm not feeling good."

"Alright." Nick stands, and they slap hands and slap each other on the back.

Wyatt holds out his hand, "Good to finally meet you, Tyler. You know this guy talks about you all the time. And though I'm not gay—"

"Not gay," Nick interjects,

"Really happy for you guys."

"You had to point out that you weren't gay to say that?"

"I'm attractive, I didn't want to give off the wrong vibe."

"Fuck you, what vibe? There's no vibe. He's not gay either."

"So you're just gay for each other?" Nick shoves him, and Wyatt's laughing. "Okay, okay, just trying to understand. Love you, bro, you know that."

"Get out of here."

"Oh no, there's that vibe—"

"There's no fucking vibe!"

Wyatts cracking up as he walks away.

"Fucker," Nick mumbles. "Come on, let's go."

Sixteen

Tyler: Kiss

I follow Nick to the car blindly.

Everything I thought was right wasn't, and now I don't know what to do. I feel guilty. I feel stupid. I don't understand why Nick had to spell it out for me to get it.

From my point of view, it's easy to see why I was confused because, technically, my ideas weren't so far-fetched. Everything we have done was because Katie wanted us to. But when I change that perspective and see Nick's side, I don't know how it wasn't visible. He has done far more than what any normal husband would do for their wife. I should have realized that at some point, he was doing things for me as well. When did it change? When did I start mattering to him?

What do I say now? Sorry? Just doesn't seem like enough. I accused him of using me. I don't know what to say to undo that.

Nick opens the door to his car, and I'm right behind him. He turns to me, confused, but I continue to step forward till I'm in his space. He glances around, but there is a truck next to us, hiding us, and then looks back at me. I take his arm, keeping him still, giving him time to push me away, but he doesn't. He allows it, and my lips rest on his. Gently at first, unsure and slow. We haven't kissed in over two weeks, and I don't know how he'll respond.

Then he cups the side of my face, kissing me back. With each gentle movement, the intensity increases until my heart is pounding. The adrenaline picks up between us, making it hard to breathe. I part only to suck in some air and then attack his lips again, my hand gliding up his side to push against his back. He keeps me against him, meeting each one of my movements, just as eager and willing. I've missed him, and I think, maybe, he missed me too.

We part, panting, his lips red and swollen, and I meet his eyes. It's so apparent now, his own desire.

Hands on my back grab my shirt and spin me until my face smashes into the hood of the car. An arm presses on my neck, pain pinching my spine.

Nick's shouting. "Martin, Stop!"

"This is bullshit, Nick. You aren't gay!"

I stare out, every moment of the attack at the restaurant repeating just like it has done every time I close my eyes. The emotions flood into all rational thoughts and drown me: the helplessness, the rage, the betrayal. My hand curls into a fist.

Martin hesitates, but the pressure begins to ease up, "Nick, I know you man, this ain't you." Martin huffs and pushes away. But that is his mistake.

I spin around and punch him in the face. He stumbles then

falls to the floor. I jump on him, punching everywhere I can hit, ignoring all the screaming Nick is doing. I won't be a bitch again. I'm winning this fucking fight. Blood splatters from his broken nose. I snatch my knife out of my pocket and flick it open, pressing it against his neck. His eyes are wide, and he's still. It's the fear I've been feeling, and now I have control over it. I want to destroy it, to destroy him and everything he represents.

Nick is at my side, "Tyler. Tyler, don't, please, let him go."

"I'm tired of his shit. I'm tired of people like him."

"I know. I am too. I'll take care of it. But he's my brother."

All I see are the faces of the men that attacked us. I'll never be able to get them out of my head.

Nick touches my back, and I shove away, pacing. Wyatt is there, and he leads me away, talking nonsense into my ear. I don't go far, keeping an eye on Nick. I won't let him forgive that asshole this time.

"This guy has something on you," Martin struggles to get back on his feet, his hands covered in blood, the liquid dripping from his chin. "He's got something on your head. I know he does. Tell me what it is, I'll fix it for you. Nick, please. You aren't gay. We grew up together."

"Why would you do this? After what we've been through. I'm still fucking healing from a stab wound from bigots like you. How are you going to do this to me?"

"You're not gay. You're not gay."

"I'm done, Martin. Stay out of my life. If you ever come near Katie or Tyler, I'm gonna fuck you up."

"We're brothers—"

"And you've ruined it. I can't deal with you. Fuck, Martin. You—" Nick shakes his head and backs away when Martin tries

95

to grab him. "You betrayed me. Again!"

"I'm your brother-"

"I should have never given you a second chance after Katie. This is my life, Martin. He's part of my life now. And if you can't be for it, or at least pretend to be, then we can't be family."

"You're gonna choose him over me? You're gonna choose your fucking boyfriend over your brother?"

Nick shakes his head, a bitter smile on his lips, "Looks like it."

Martin pounds the hood of Nick's car, "That's bullshit." He points to me, eyes full of hate, "I'm gonna figure it out. I'm gonna find out. You ain't fooling me."

I'm yelling right back, "It's all out on the table, man, come on! You want to fucking fight me? Let's go!"

"Get out of here," Nick orders.

Martin pulls the door on his truck, the very one next to us. I should have known it was his fucking car. Dicks like him usually drive pickups. "I'm telling dad."

Nick laughs, "Go ahead. He gave me his blessing this morning. You can't stop this. We're getting married!"

"I'm not gonna let that happen. I'm not."

Nick opens his mouth to reply but then sways and grabs hold of the car. I shove out of Wyatt's grip and run to Nick as he lowers to the ground. He holds his head, concentrating entirely on breathing.

Martin comes to the other side, "Nick? Nick."

Nick looks at me, "I'm tired."

"Let's go home," I wrap his arm around me and lift him.

Martin attempts to help, but Nick pushes his arm away, "Get out of here, Martin. I don't want to see you again."

Seventeen

Tyler: Hotter

Katie holds my hand in hers, gently applying Neosporin to the cut on my knuckles. It's the third time this year that she's tended to the same damn wound, in the same damn spot. It's like it won't heal. She's upset, but she doesn't say it.

The phone next to us rings, and she clicks off again. It's the fifth phone call in the last twenty minutes. Nick's family is trying to figure out what happened, but she doesn't want to talk to them yet.

I told her everything. I made it clear that it wasn't my fault, but for some reason, I don't think she believes me. It might be because I am typically the instigator.

Dinner is cold on the table. Nick is asleep upstairs. And it's quiet. It's like the calm before the storm.

She slaps down the gauze, pressing it a little harder than necessary, and then wraps it up.

"It wasn't my fault."

"It never is," She replies dryly.

I clench my teeth, turning away.

"You know how Martin is. You kissed Nick right in front of him. You provoked him."

"I didn't even know he was there."

"Sure."

"I didn't."

She snaps shut the medical kit, bringing it back to the cabinet, and then slams that shut, "Nick is still recovering—"

"I know."

"I'm just over all this fighting."

"You think I'm not?"

Katie scoffs, "No. I think you want to fight. I think you're angry, and instead of talking about it, you're resorting to violence."

"That's not true."

"Tell that to the wall upstairs."

I get to my feet, "What do you want me to do?"

"Talk to someone! Anyone. Honey, you were attacked. You have every right to be mad, but you have to let it out. You have to let it go."

"How do I do that? Let it go? Everyone's telling me that's what I need to do, but no one is telling me how."

"Forgive."

The words brings disgust to my lips, "Forgive? Forgive those assholes for nearly killing Nick? Have you forgiven them?"

The phone rings again, and she grabs it, "Hello?" She forces a calm voice, but every tension in her body says otherwise. "He's sleeping. I'll have him call you when he wakes up." She places it back down, staring off before she gets her breath. Katie comes to me, touching my cheek, and I lean into it, closing my eyes. "I'm just worried about you."

Following her lead, I calm down and take a seat. With a little gesture, she comes to me and I pull her between my legs, "You don't need to worry. I'll go to the gym; I'll beat the crap out of a punching bag."

"You practically live at the gym."

Guilt is thick. I'm done with my doctor's appointments this month, but it doesn't make it any better. It's a lie on my tongue that is pulling me down. "You don't get a body like this with magic."

Katie holds me close, her head on my shoulder. "Are you guys better now?"

She makes me think of the kiss between Nick and me. The rare moment where it is only about the two of us. It's impossible to hold back the smile, "Yeah."

"Did he say it?"

"Kind of."

"Tell me everything."

"He just made me see what I was missing. I thought everything he was doing was for you. But I was wrong."

"I knew it. Didn't I tell you?"

"It's different coming from him. No offense, but you think the deer in the back are your friends."

"Do they come up to anyone else's porch?"

I chuckle, and she snuggles into my neck.

"Nick told me you asked him to marry you. I don't think I've ever told you how brave you are."

"Me?"

She nods into my skin.

I don't see what she sees, but I'm not gonna fight it. I like that she sees something good in me.

"So we're all getting married. How insane is that?"

"Or stressful."

"Right now. It will get better."

"Is this normal? To have all this going on?"

I'm tired of all the mayhem. I want a quiet day where nothing goes wrong. I don't fight anyone. I don't want to have any arguments. I just want peace.

Katie runs her fingers through my hair, "It won't always be crazy. It will be slow and easy. That's the time it gets boring. The time when people look for other ways to get excited."

I pull back with my brows knit, "You talking about cheating?"

She shrugs, keeping her eyes down, "I think everybody can cheat. I think you're gorgeous and sexy and young, and I'm fifteen years older than you, and I can't get pregnant—"

I stand with her in my arms, gripping her cheeks, forcing her to look up at me. "I love you. I've already had enough fun. I want boring. I'm ready for life to be simple and easy and to know every day I'm coming home to you and Nick."

"And if we never have a baby?"

I rest my forehead against hers, "I will be fine, Katie. The question is, will you be?" She sniffs and doesn't answer.

She feels the way I did, wanting something that might not ever come. I at least got my happy ending. I'm going to work my ass off to give her hers. I grip the back of her head, kissing her with terrible desperation.

I got one more month to put a baby inside her before I leave for my internship. Until then, every day, Katie's going to have cum dripping out of her pussy.

* * *

I rub my eyes, sitting at my desk. I stayed up all night. Half the time, I was making love to Katie while the other half spent stressing over Nick. He didn't wake up the whole night. It's been over twelve hours, the sun is beginning to rise, and he continues to sleep.

I have to fill out paperwork for my new job at John F. Kennedy in Philadelphia. I don't know how I'm going to commute. It's a two-hour drive. We were talking about moving, but I haven't heard of any such plans in weeks. With the HOA threatening to kick us out, I think it's a great opportunity, but once again, no one has said anything. I could apply to a closer hospital, but crappy little hospitals aren't a place to make a name. I'll just be another doctor. Plus, the more popular the hospital, the more money I'll make, and if I ever want to pay off Nick in this lifetime, I need to make the most I can.

I flex my fingers; my knuckles hurt with the familiar ache. The gauze is tight. I peel at the tape, slowly removing it to reveal the broken red skin.

Katie is right. I'm not myself.

I scared myself yesterday, pressing the knife up against Martin's neck. I had every intention of slicing his skin. It would have been easy like using a scalpel. I know just the right amount of pressure to break the skin or to dig through muscle and tendon. I've never practiced on a real person. They only supply dummies in school. The blood would be real, warm and sticky.

I close my eyes, breathing in deep, holding it, before I let it out. Forgiving those assholes isn't something I can do. There has to be another way to let all this rage go.

A knock on my door turns my head, and Nick crosses his arms as he leans against the wall.

"Hey, you okay?" I ask quickly.

"Yeah. I'm hungry but good."

I know he's got something to say about the fight between Martin and me. I've been waiting for it.

"Where'd you get the knife?"

"I bought it."

"Why?"

I shrug. I feel guilty, but I'm also justified. I needed to use it, and this time I had it.

"Give it to me."

I clench my teeth and ignore him.

He comes into my room, snatching my laundry basket and digging in it, looking for the jeans I wore yesterday, "Where is it?"

"You think I'm gonna sit back next time and watch them kill you? Or let them kill me?"

Nick points a finger in my face, "You are a doctor. You don't take a life, you hear me? You save it."

"You're acting like it's a fucking gun. Pretty hypocritical."

"I'm trained, I'm licensed, I won't go to jail for protecting myself. But you will. For manslaughter. For murder. And I'm not out for revenge. Now give it to me."

"No."

"Tyler. You give it to me, or you get out of this house."

I shake my head, staring at the computer screen.

"I know you're angry. I am too. But vengeance is not our place."

"You sound like your dad."

"What's wrong with that? He's right. Please. Don't be stupid. Give me the knife."

I snap open the drawer next to me. Nick takes the knife and

disappears.

I'll just get another one. He's not going to stop me from protecting us against the fucking haters out there. I'm going to be useful next time.

Nick comes back and sits on the bed, but I don't pay attention. I pretend to work, typing, but I don't know what I'm writing.

"I'm sorry." He murmurs. "It's my job to protect you and Katie, and I failed—"

"What?" I turn to him, "Why is it your job?"

"Because I'm…"

"A man? What the fuck am I?"

Nick gawks, shrugging, struggling to come up with something. He looks like an idiot.

I lean back, rolling my eyes, "Why am I seen as the fucking woman in this? Everyone at work thought you were the one that took it in the ass, just to let you know."

"What? Why? You are way more emotional than I am."

"Because I'm a sex icon."

He makes a gross face, "To who?"

"To every woman that has ever laid eyes on me. To every writer that's ever written a sex book. Or to every director that's ever made a porno."

"That's a damn lie. I'm way hotter than you."

"How do you see that?"

"Aside from just being better looking, I'm Spanish."

"So?"

"So? That's the appeal. I'm the Spanish lover everyone wants. Number two, I'm a beast." He flexes his bicep. "That's all muscle. My bicep is the size of your damn thigh."

"First, not all muscle, be honest. And second, I'm fit. You're like a cement truck while I'm Ferrari."

"If I'm any car, I'm a Ford Super Duty F-450."

"Most women don't want trucks. And plus, you're hairy as fuck; you're like Godzilla."

"Hair is in. You look like a ken doll."

"Hair is so *not* in. I think I know the market better than you."

"'The market'? That's so fucked up."

"Case in point, you're old."

"Fuck you; I look like I'm twenty."

"No, I look like I'm twenty. You look like you're forty."

"See, now I know you're lying."

"Forty can be hot. But you ain't twenty, that's for damn sure."

"Case in point, age is wisdom. And knowledge is hot."

"I'm a doctor. You've been fucked this whole conversation." I spin in my chair, proud I've won.

"In training. I own two restaurants and make 300 grand a year. What's your paycheck?" He claps his hands, standing, "Winner!" He hollers. Then he pauses, "And you're the girl because you take it in the ass." He's laughing, trying to dodge out the door.

I holler after him, "That can change at any time."

Nick peeks back in, "No, it really can't."

Katie leans beside him, dressed in her pajamas, "What's going on in here?" she yawns.

"Katie, who's hotter, me or Tyler?"

Her eyes widen, and then she spins around, "Coming, Mom!"

Eighteen

Tyler: Cleared

I'm learning that dating a man is similar to hanging out with one. Video games is our 'Love Language' apparently because that is how Nick and I have been spending our time, healing weeks of damage.

Our relationship has finally gotten some ground. The last four weeks were thankfully stress-free. I'm out of school, Nick is out of work till he heals, and Katie is home, so we have all gotten to spend a ton of quality time together, which is something that's been overdue.

All should be perfect, right? I should be sleeping at night. I should be able to get out of the house and not be looking over my shoulder. I should be able to laugh and have fun with my girlfriend and boyfriend and not be bothered by anything.

But I'm struggling. I'm struggling to get my head away from the violence we went through. I can't stop thinking about it—nightmare after nightmare. When we are out in public, I'm looking for faces. I'm searching for judgment. I won't touch Nick when someone's around. I can no longer risk it.

I'm getting help. Marco is going to help me find the guy that stabbed Nick. I'm meeting up with someone tonight. It's all going to end.

I'm going to end it.

Snowball jumps off my lap and runs to the door. Nick had gone to the doctor's for his last checkup, and Katie went with her sister for a dress fitting. I'm sitting here watching the clock, waiting till I have to get moving. David is going with me, though he doesn't know why I'm insisting on Dave and Buster's.

The door pops open, and Nick walks in, laughing at Snowball as she jumps up, trying to lick his face. "Hey!"

I throw the controller, getting up, "Hey, man, how'd the doctor's go?"

Nick doesn't say hello. He comes at me like a bull, grabbing my face and slamming his lips against mine. I'm not ready for it, and I stumble backward, falling against the armrest of the couch. He kisses my chin, my jaw, attacking my neck while he grabs my hips, pushing me against him. His hard-on is thick and ready against my thigh. "Doc said I'm good." He breathlessly mumbles against my neck.

"Good? Meaning you can have sex?"

"Hmm hmm." Nick steps back just to take off his shirt and then kisses me deep, his tongue digging into my mouth. A rush of excitement drops in my belly, and I'm eager, gripping him with as much vigor. We haven't even made out since we've made up, and now I want to make up for all the lost time.

Making out with Nick is harder to accomplish because, as I've said, I'm not turned on by Nick. Where I can make out with Katie any time or any day of the week, it takes a bit more effort with Nick, and most of the time, I'd rather just play a game or go to the gym. We show affection in different ways than physical.

But his intensity is pulling that desire out of me. My blood is pumping fast, and it's all flowing to my dick.

We fall on the couch. He's on top, grinding his solid cock into me. "I'm gonna fuck you both in the ass." He moans, nipping at my skin. He's never been so openly sexual with me. It's making me horny as fuck.

"I'm gonna make you cum this time with my dick inside you. Fuck, I want to cum right now." He leans back on his knees, unbuckling his pants. I'm panting with excitement, watching, waiting for what he'll do next. "Katie! Get down here," he hollers, pulling out his thick, long dick.

Nick falls on me again. "I want you to suck my cock," he grinds into me, biting my neck. "I want it down your throat."

I hate to say it because I know what's going to happen, but I can't let Nick keep going. "Katie's not here."

Nick pulls back. "What? Where is she?"

"She left with her sister an hour ago. Dress fitting."

He sits back on his heels. "Oh," he looks down at his cock, a horribly awkward moment before he shoves it back in, getting up. "Well, ah… I'm gonna go shower."

"Ni—"

He runs upstairs.

I sit up, scratching my head, feeling guilty. Maybe I should have told him when he first walked in, but I didn't know he was going to be horny, in my defense. I'm sure he's not ready for a full-on gay session, and I don't know if I am either. Katie brings a lot to the table. Her pussy for one, her breasts, her mouth, her moans, her soul.

I chew on my lip and look at my phone. If I play our videos on the TV, it won't be a hundred percent gay. And he did say he likes when I push, so maybe, if I push just a little, I could give him the relief he's looking for. Not full-on ass fucking, but I could at least suck his cock and maybe get him to suck mine.

Our first time and only time doing things without Katie was a couple of years ago, and that left Nick questioning his orientation and was a complete ass for months.

Should I risk it?

I jump up on my feet and take the stairs two at a time.

In the bathroom, Nick stands in the spray, and upon seeing me, his eyes are wide. I undress and open the door.

"What are you doing?"

I step into the water, pulling him to me, and kiss him. He responds, but he also pushes me a little, "Tyler, we can't."

I'm kissing his jaw and down his neck, "It's alright. Pretend she's out there." I kiss him again, and he copies every move I make, his lips molding into mine. "She's tied up on the bed." With the hot water spraying on us, I reach down between us to hold his cock, jerking him, "Her pussy's wet." He grips my ass, holding me close, the other hand on the back of my neck, to keep my lips playing with his. He groans, his hips flexing with each jerk. "Her hard nipples, begging to be pinched." I grab the soap and pour it on our hard dicks. With one hand, I keep them connected, the soap making it the right amount of slippery.

"A vibrator in her ass," he adds, breathless watching our cocks rubbing together. I kiss his neck and shoulders. His hand rubs down my back, gripping my ass once again before he smacks it hard. Then it comes around and grabs my cock. He jerks me, and I close my eyes, throwing my head back, jerking him.

"Suck me," he orders.

I drop to my knees and take him in. He puts his hands against the wall, thrusting into my mouth long, slow movements. It's not long until one of his hands comes down, pressing against the back of my head, gripping my hair, and increasing his pace with intensity. He is eager after all these weeks. He is rough, careless when he chokes me with his fat cock down my throat. I spit him out, coughing, getting my breath back.

"Come on. I know you can take it deep."

I bite his ball sack. He groans, squeezing my hair, enjoying it more than I thought he would. I take him in again and tilt my head back, meeting his eyes as he dips his dick all the way to the back of my throat. His mouth hangs open, and his eyes squeeze shut. I hold him there for an extra second before I pull him out, only to do it again. He pants heavy, and I hear him whisper, "God, I missed this."

Snowball is barking downstairs. Nick grips my arm, pulling me up in a panic, "Katie's home." He shuts off the shower, and we are out, dripping wet on the tile, acting like we were teenagers caught making out when our parents come home. He tosses me a towel and wraps one around him before going out.

I watch him get dressed as I wrap the towel around my waist. I'm confused about why he's rushing. "You know Katie would love it if she found us, right?"

Katie walks in, "Hey!"

"Hey!" Nick greets her in his boxers, hugging her and glaring at me over her shoulder. It's a subtle threat. I smirk, leaning up against the doorway, wondering if I do tell her what he'll do about it.

"Have fun with your sister?"

"Oh my god! What a nut," Katie collapses on the bed, "She loves to complain."

"She's your mother."

"She is, right? Am I like my mom?"

"No, baby, not even close."

"Thank god. I think I'd turn myself into the loony bin had you said yes."

She tilts her head back and notices me in a towel. She lifts her head toward Nick, "Were you guys taking a shower together?"

Nick's eyes widen, and then he announces, "I'm gonna make dinner," he leaves the room still only dressed in his boxers.

I lean over Katie, kissing her while she's upside down, reaching for a breast, squeezing, then sliding down to grab her vagina. "Go spread your legs for Nick. Think he needs that pussy."

"He's been cleared? Finally!" she dashes out the door.

I stick my head out the door, making sure she's downstairs before I shut it, flicking the lock. In the closet, behind a pile of medical books, I pull out a blue bag. My medications jiggle as I dig around, searching for the one I need now. I have to take three different kinds and at alternating times of the day. It's annoying and hard to remember, but I've been doing it for the last two weeks. Side effects are kicking my ass, though. I'm finding it harder to have sex, but that could also be because of the PTSD I seem to have.

I'm going to tell them everything soon. Once I have the name of Nick's attacker, and I get my revenge, I'll come clean about it all. I'll deal with the consequences. But I need to go to them with a solution. I have to show Katie and Nick and myself I'm not some punk-ass bitch that can be taken down so fucking quickly.

Nineteen

Tyler: Sinking

I hop down the last stair and find Katie and Nick on the couch. She's riding him like she mounted a horse, her breasts bouncing, her moans chaotic. I get out my phone and record her. She doesn't know how beautiful and sexy she is. Or maybe she does because she looks at me with her hooded eyes, leaning her hands back on Nick's knees, pushing her big breasts further out, rotating her hips back and forth in a gentle swinging motion.

I move toward them with the camera in front, lowering it between Nick's legs to record his dick sinking to her pussy. He grips her ass, spreading her cheeks, exposing her asshole.

"Join us," Katie whimpers.

I run a hand along Katie's ass, admiring it like it's the dark side of the moon. "I'm meeting up with someone." My hand dips down, stroking Nick's balls.

My middle finger lines up with his cock, and it slides into Katie's pussy with him. Once my finger is juiced up, I stick it in her lonely asshole. She bucks and looks back, grabbing my wrist, moving me the way she wants it.

"I got to go."

"No," She keeps hold of my hand, "Stay, baby."

I take a ball full of her hair and tilt her head back, "Don't tell me what to do." She grins, straining against my hold. I'd love to fuck her, but I'm way too anxious about tonight to get it up. She'll have to be satisfied with my hand. I pound my finger into her ass, and her mouth falls open, gasping, moaning. Just before she cums, I pull out, smacking her ass.

"You're still leaving?"

"I'll be back in a couple hours," I lean over the couch and kiss Nick, "Don't get too tired. You made a lot of promises earlier."

"What promises?" Katie wonders.

I smile into his mouth, and he whispers, "Asshole."

* * *

It's a half-hour drive to Dave and Buster's and David's waiting for me at the front door.

"You're late."

"Your sister takes time." I hold up two fingers, wagging them in front of his face.

David slaps it like it's poison and stumbles away, "God, you're a dick."

"I washed my hands," I slap him on the back, and he winces in disgust. "Let's get drunk."

"You're buying."

"Nick's buying," I wink, laughing.

David and I have become close since the attack. He's been my outlet. I vent to him about every bullshit thing that's happened. Ray and him are the only ones that know about my recent diagnoses, and since Ray lives far, David's come with me to a couple of appointments.

We sit at the bar. I'm trying to get him a girl, but so far, it's been no luck. There's a bunch of nerdy-looking women, but I want a slut for him. They either don't come here (which is obvious), or they are already with a guy. "We need to go to a strip joint."

"You're the one that suggested Dave and Buster's. And I'm not taking my sister's fiance to a strip joint. She'd kill me. What about that one?" He flicks his head to the right.

"She's a little fat."

"Jeeze, you're picky. She's perfect. I don't expect anorexic. And what about personality?"

"You're cute. Personality. Do people like you really exist?"

"It's not all about sex."

"It's a lot to do with it."

"That's good to hear since you're marrying my sister."

"I love Katie. But you're not looking for love, are you?"

David shrugs. "It would be nice to have someone to talk to."

"You got me," he chuckles. I nudge him, whispering, "The girl in green."

He looks over at her, wincing, "She's got to be in her twenties."

"Prime pussy. Old enough to know how to work a cock. Young enough that her pussy's not stretched out by all the dick."

David covers his face.

113

I slap his shoulder, "Alright, alright, I'll calm it down."

"That's another problem. No girl is going to look at me with you sitting here."

I notice a guy sit down across the bar, and I nod in greeting. He rotates on his seat and leaves. "I'll leave you to it, bro. Go say hi."

"And then what?"

"Do what we talked about. Tell her you want to fuck."

"Oh god."

I'm laughing and sipping my drink as I move into the crowd. I find the guy standing next to a high top, and I maneuver over to him. "Marco's friend."

He tosses a piece of paper on the table. "That's the name."

I pick it up, leaving behind an envelope, and put the paper in my pocket. When he picks up the envelope, I notice the tattoo on his hand. It's a symbol I've become very familiar with over the past few weeks. My body flushes with rage. "You're AFA."

"And be sure to know, I know where you live, so if they find out who ratted him out, I'm coming for you."

"Why are you turning in your own man?"

"Hate the guy. Plus, money is good. But if you want to know who ordered the attack, it's a different price."

I'm confused with what he means at first. I watch him as he walks away. But I notice him going into the family bathroom. The insinuation isn't lost. He wants me to suck his dick. The fucker is gay and in the AFA. He hunts his own fucking kind.

My breath is wild; my heart is pounding. I could suck his dick, get a name, get revenge. It wouldn't be real cheating, right? There is a reason behind it. I'm not doing it for pleasure. I'm not doing it for me. I'd be doing it for us. To get the guys that jumped us off the street. We'd be safe. It would be like a job.

I down my drink and take a step toward it. Nick and Katie would never have to know. I could get away with it. I know how to keep secrets.

"So that didn't work." David comes up out of nowhere, and I flinch, turning to him. "You alright?"

I grip the table with my eyes on the bathroom. He's still there. Waiting. I can say I'm going to the bathroom, and there would be no question or concern.

David continues, "I'm no good at small talk. Let's try somewhere else. These girls are too young. I feel like I'm hitting on someone's daughter. Well, I guess I am, but you know what I mean. You alright? You look pale."

"No, no, let's go."

I follow him, eyeing the door. What if it pisses him off? What if he sets the AFA after us out of bitterness?

"I gotta go to the bathroom."

"Oh, yeah, me too."

As we approach, the door opens. The man walks by me, and I keep my head straight, trying to keep breathing, trying to keep the sound of my pounding heart from reaching anyone else.

I close my eyes, and I don't know what the hell just happened, but I'm fucked up from it.

Twenty

Tyler: Wet

When I get home, despite having told them to wait, I'm disappointed that they actually did. After my confused run-in, I'm too much in my head. They're in the hot tub, both naked. I stand on the other side of the sliding glass door, watching them talk, drinking wine, staring up at the stars.

What would I do if I lost them?

Where would I go?

Who would I be?

All the struggle that I've gone through to keep them in my life would have been for nothing. The past three years would have been tossed in the garbage. And it would have been my fault. I'd live with that regret for the rest of my life.

I have to tell them. I can't keep trying to keep my head above water by myself. I need help.

I slide open the door, and both of them turn to me with a smile,

"He returns!" Nick exaggerates.

Katie stands up, and the water glistens off her body. It's the perfect porno movie where they slow it down, playing some cheesy romantic music in the background. Her nipples are hard in the center of her perfectly shaped breasts. The light adds shadows to the right spots, enhancing her stomach muscles and her toned thighs. How is it possible that I've fucked her so many times, and she still turns me on?

Katie gets out of the tub and pulls me out of the doorway. Her hands are on my belt. I watch her, unmoving, allowing her to undress me in an effort to clear my head. I used to be so good at switching off my thoughts and just fucking when I have to, but it's been so long since I've done a job, I don't think I could do it anymore. The fact that I couldn't go through with sucking dick in the bathroom is proof.

She's changed me. She's domesticated me.

Katie pulls down my pants. I kick out of my shoes and step out of my pants. Her hand skims over my flaccid penis before she pulls off my shirt. She takes my hand and leads me to the tub. Her ass is in my sight, the plump thick piece of fat. I can't help but reach out and grab it. Katie pauses on the steps to lean over, sticking her ass out so that I could slap it.

She lives to be fucked. And I live to fuck her.

The hot tub is always a reminder of how we started. She had been in Nick's arms, scared and nervous. I was sitting across from them, simply watching as they made out. Now she sits on my lap, and Nick is the one watching, stroking his cock.

We make out, my hands riding up her back and down to grip her ass. I rub her pussy against my dick.

"I've watched you guys enough these past six weeks. You do the watching." Nick grabs her arm and pulls her off me to kiss her himself. She wraps her arms around him, but I'm not sitting by. I move up behind her, twisting my fingers in her hair and forcing her to turn to me. Her tongue is out, and I flick my own across her. Nick adds his. I turn my attention to him, kissing him.

Nick and I both stand-up. Our cocks pointing at each other with Katie between us. We're making out while Katie grabs our dicks, our tips brushing against her lips. I feel like we haven't had a threesome in years. I'm crazily excited, forgetting all about tonight. I want to do everything, every position we can think of, no matter how long it takes.

We watch her take us in one dick at a time. Katie sucks me and jerks Nick off, then switches. Her head bobs over his dick. I grab her hair, forcing her deeper, to the point of making her gag. She glares at me, but I lean down and kiss her, wagging my tongue against hers. Nick pushes his cock between us, and I give in, swallowing him but only a few times before I let Katie go back to sucking us off.

I'm ready to eat that pussy now. I lift her, sitting her on the edge of the tub, spreading her legs. Nick grabs one ankle while I have the other. Katie rubs her pussy for us, and we jerk off for her. She dips a finger inside and then holds it up. Nick snags it and sucks on it. I get my own, shoving two fingers into her; her mouth opens in a gasp. I pull them out to suck, and she watches with desire in her hooded gaze. I do it again, but Nick grabs my hand, sucking it off my finger. I pull him in, my tongue swirling inside his mouth, getting the last taste of pussy. His hand slides on my back, gripping my ass, slapping me.

I drop down and lick Katie's vagina from bottom to top,

ending at her clit where I draw circles with my tongue. She flinches and gasps. Nick's hand slides up and down my back while he kisses Katie's leg and my shoulder. His fingers slide between my buttcheeks and press into my asshole, but it's momentary. It's a tease, a hint of where tonight is going to go. It increases my energy, and I take it out on her pussy, my tongue buried into her. I want Nick to do whatever he wants, but I'm not going to push. I'm gonna let him lead and reap the benefits of his desires.

Nick slips a finger inside me. He knows how to find my prostate by now, and he presses into it. My hips jerk on reflex. He is gentle, his finger scratching at the sweet spot, and I'm panting into Katie's vagina. Pleasure stretches to all nerves, and my legs shake under the duress. I grab my cock, nearly ready to cum already. Thankfully Nick notices and backs out, slapping my ass. I break from Katie and kiss him, trying to explain I want more without talking. I know how much he hates it, but sometimes it's hard to keep quiet, to keep from demanding. I wonder what he would do if I told him to fuck me right now.

We eat Katie's pussy together. My hand is all over him, just like he is all over me. We keep making out with Katie's juices on our lips.

In the water, my legs and Nick's intertwine, our dicks rubbing. He's constantly gripping my ass and sliding a finger against my asshole, sending a wave of anticipation through me.

Katie stands up, and I lay back with my head against the edge of the tub. She sits on my face and nearly suffocates me with her vagina. I keep my tongue out, and she grinds her lips against it. Nick comes between my legs to eat her out from behind. He presses between my legs, his dick against mine, dry humping, rocking the water, as he tongues her asshole. My heels dig into his thighs, forcing him harder and harder. Our dicks can do nothing else but rub on each other.

"So quiet tonight." She murmurs.

I slap her ass, "That loud enough for you?

She shoves me with a smile, sitting down beside me. Nick is kissing my neck, and I shift my head, bringing his lips up to mine. He sucks at all the leftovers of Katie's cum. I grip his arms, keeping him close. He continuously thrusts against me, the water rocking with his movements. Katie keeps her hands on us, encouraging our bisexual encounter. His lips move down my chin, and he bites my neck.

"I got to go to the bathroom," Katie announces, getting up.

It breaks Nick's concentration, and he pulls back, sitting across from me now. He continues stroking himself with his head leaned back against the railing.

It's time to push a little.

I move through the water and crawl on his lip, straddling his waist.

I kiss him, rotating my hips so once more, our dicks are stroking themselves. He grips my ass, squeezing both cheeks, pulling me close. I break from our kiss, "You gonna fuck me?"

"Why do you got to talk?" He leans his head back, dropping his hands away. But I don't get off. I lean up on my knees, reach behind me to grab his cock.

He snaps his head up, "What are you doing?"

I press his dick to my asshole, "You want me too?"

He grits his teeth, panting through his nose.

I lower, just an inch.

He grabs my hips, "Fuck." His nails dig into my skin as he struggles between pushing me away and pounding into me. I can see every emotion on his face. He wants to, but he can't.

Katie returns, and I release him, slipping off him. "It's so fucking hot watching you two." She comes to Nick's side, and his arm wraps around her. He kisses her and then kisses me, and then I kiss her. Her hand is between us, randomly stroking each of us.

"Ride me, baby." Nick orders, pulling her onto his cock. I watch as she sinks on his dick, her chest puffed out with her hands on his knees. She's slow, so fucking slow it doesn't even jar the water. I want her to get plowed. I want her screaming.

When my turn comes up, I flip Katie over, and her ass sticks up out of the water as she hangs over the edge of the spa. I smack her. Again. And Again. And Again. Her ass is bright red and beautiful. I kiss my marks like trophies. I wrap a hand around her neck, pulling her up against my chest. And as I squeeze, I dive into her pussy. Every thrust is hard, and her moans sound choked. I screw her harshly; water splashes all around us. I don't stop till we both are cumming.

It's not long before we are done with the tub and want our bed. We head upstairs, and I know when we get to that room, it's no longer going to be about Katie's desires but mine.

Twenty-One

Tyler: Full

I snatch a vibrator from the nightstand before I lay down on the bed. Katie snuggles into me, looking at my face, "So…" she begins, "You guys going to…you know?"

"It's all Nick."

"Oh, he's ready."

"Then me too."

"You ever think we'd get here?"

"Did I ever imagine I'd let a man fuck me in the ass? Hmm, let me think."

Katie giggles, kissing my chin. "But you're happy, right? You're not doing this for me?"

I brush hair out of her face, "I told you how I feel about Nick. I'm doing this for me."

"It's crazy. Nick was the straightest guy in the world. But you changed him. Like you changed me. I'm so happy you are in my life."

"You'll be even happier if you were sitting on my face."

Katie grins wickedly, crawling over me and kneeling over my shoulders. We sixty-nine, waiting for Nick, who decided he was hungry all of a sudden. I get it; he's nervous, so we both let him go without saying anything.

I roll the vibrator between her pussy lips, getting it nice and wet before I drag it up to her asshole. Her body jerks as it reaches the outer rim. I tease her, taking it away, resting it on her thigh, dragging it up till it touches once more. She groans around my cock, "Please."

I'll always give in to her begging. I slip it in. Her ministrations become chaotic as she loses her concentration while her pleasure increases. With my feet on the bed, I fuck her mouth from the bottom, thrusting up into her open lips.

Nick's hands rest on my knees, and I stop my movement. Sliding his hands down to my thighs, he folds my legs toward my hips. Katie stops sucking, meeting his lips, and they kiss above my twitching cock. It hits Katie in the chin, beckoning. She lowers the both of them till their tongues are flicking over my tip. I don't want to close my eyes, watching the two of them play with my cock between them. Katie sucks, and then Nick. It's such a rarity, like shooting star rarity, that Nick sucks cock.

Katie encourages him, "I love watching you do that."

He leaves me and kisses her, "Only for you."

If it were only for her, he wouldn't do anymore, but he drops his head back down to flick his tongue over my balls. I slap Katie's ass to control my moans. He's getting closer to my ass, and my breathing picks up like I'm running a damn marathon. I'm nervous and excited, like a virgin on his wedding night.

When Nick's tongue dives into my asshole, I drop from

Katie's pussy, clenching my eyes shut, instinctively spreading my legs further apart. He spreads my asscheeks, digging his tongue in deep. Katie removes my dick from her mouth, sucking on my balls, licking down my chode, meeting Nick's tongue occasionally. It's fucking heaven, and I lay there enjoying their ministrations.

Then a vibrator is inside my ass. I bite Katie's thigh in retaliation. I slap her ass, taking out my aggression on her. I twitch and jerk as he rotates it around. He hits my prostate like a fucking pro, and I nearly reach down to grab it, "Stop, stop, stop. I don't want to cum."

Katie pops my dick out of her mouth and tongues the tip. Nick removes the vibrator, and I can breathe again. I thought I was going to shoot my load already. I'm panting, staring at the ceiling with Katie's pussy an inch from my face.

The cold lube shocks me, and I'm lifting my head out from under Katie's leg to see what he is doing. He sticks a lube-covered finger into my ass as he jerks his cock with the liquid. He's on his knees on the bed between my legs. My breath is in a panic, and I swallow, clenching my eyes shut, holding onto Katie's leg.

When she moves to go, I almost yank her back. Nick and I haven't fucked in months. It's going to hurt just like it did last time, and now I know how much it hurts, so it's hard to stay put. Katie turns and sits on my cock. I pop my eyes open, surprised. She smiles down at me, leaning over to make out with me as she bounces. Her big breasts are smacking me in the chin, keeping my attention.

Nick grabs my legs, pushing them forward from behind the knee. I feel his cock at my asshole. He teases it first, rubbing his tip against it, the lube making it slippery.

He presses in. My mouth drops open, and a gasp escapes. Katie doesn't stop, her pussy stroking me. It keeps the pleasure coming even during a very uncomfortable moment. He keeps going. I punch the bed, caught between stopping him and wanting him.

"I'm in," he huffs, breathless, "fuck." He flexes his hips.

My mouth falls open, "Ah. Shit." I can't stop the sounds I'm making. Pleasure and pain all mixed up. He's only an inch in, and it already feels like too much, but I want more because I want him. I want us to be able to do this. I got to get through it. "Go. Go." I beg.

He is slow, going in and out, and I can only lay there, mouth open, barely breathing. After a few minutes, I relax, and the pain disappears. Pleasure is finally overriding my senses. I can handle it. I know he'll want to go deeper, but I'm happy with where we are. He grabs Katie's hips forcing her to bounce hard and fast, trying to take my attention away. I make myself move, reaching up to grab her breasts. I can open my eyes now. Katie is just watching me, so fascinated by my pleasure. I smile, but it falls as Nick slips in, just an inch more.

"How's it feel?" Katie wonders.

There's only one word that comes to mind, "Stuffed."

Katie looks behind her. Nick and her kiss. His movements increase, desperate to get his whole 9-inch cock in me. Moans breach my lips no matter how hard I clench them shut. I can't keep quiet; even my breathing is noisy.

Katie gets off. I can't stop her or reach for her. I'm paralyzed under him. He grips my ankles, keeping my legs spread as his hips move back and forth. I grab my cock, jerking, but Nick spits into his hand and takes over, jerking my cock as he fucks me. Katie is beside us, a vibrator on her pussy as she watches.

I want to help her, but I can't do anything.

Nick pulls out, and the pressure releases. Breath comes back. All my muscles relax. I'm panting, partly thankful but wondering what happened. I open my eyes to see why. He is still leaning over me, but his attention is on eating Katie's pussy. I take this time to recover, knowing it won't be long till he goes back in. There's not so much pain anymore. It's the overwhelming pressure inside that makes it uncomfortable. I can still enjoy it, but it's a lot. It's because of his long, fat dick. Had he been the size of a pickle, I'd be able to take it. But I just need to get used to it. We need to fuck more.

With pussy juice on his lips, he bends down and swallows my cock. It's a great fucking sight, and I don't want to look away. He looks awkward doing it. I can tell he doesn't like it, but he does it anyway. Only a couple sucks before he stands up, tossing my leg to the side, "Get on your knees," Nick instructs.

My legs are numb, but I roll over and get up on my hands and knees. He's behind me and slips his cock back in.

I smack the bed, gritting my teeth, grabbing the blanket to bury my face in it. "Fuck, fuck."

"Too much?" I shake my head as he goes slow. I don't want him to back out, but it's a fucking struggle. He builds up once more, one inch and then another and then a third. He slaps my ass, "We're getting there."

I grab Katie's ankle and pull her to me so my face can bury into her pussy. The vibrator continues to buzz on her clit, and I'm licking up the juices it causes.

I can't do it for long, and I end up resting my head on her thigh, watching her please herself in front of my face. I'm panting, trying to keep from collapsing. I reach a hand back, gripping Nick's hip, feeling every thrust he makes. I know he wants it harder. I know he's holding himself back. There will be a day when I beg him to fuck me as hard as he can, but it's not today.

Nick pulls out, "Lay back down."

I gladly flop down beside Katie. Nick is sweating, and he grabs a towel from the bathroom, wiping his forehead. "I need to work out more." He jokes, getting on his knees on the bed. He pushes my legs up to my chest and slips in. No longer starting from the beginning. He puts half his cock in. I throw my head back, unable to breathe, to speak, to think. I grip his arm, a warning. It's like a strong hit of cocaine. Enough to knock you over but not enough to keep you from coming back for more.

"Katie, can you get me water?"

Nick doesn't stop when she leaves, and I don't make him stop. He drops his hands beside my head, lowering, and the position changes. It's more intimate, more intimidating, and deeper. My legs are against his arms. He's a foot away from my face, and his breath hits me with each heavy huff. I force my eyes open to look at him. His brows knit in concentration. He meets my gaze for a brief moment before he clenches them shut. I know that look. He's enjoying every fucking bit of it.

I grab the back of his head and kiss him.

We are making out as he fucks me. It's intense and amazing. Nick breaks from me, breathless, "Oh fuck." He leans back on his knees, watching his cock bury into me. "I knew you could take it." Nick slaps my thigh, smiling only briefly till his mouth falls open in bold pleasure. I'm jerking my cock; his pleasure is like an aphrodisiac. I can finally feel an orgasm approaching.

"Go, go go," I grip my dick harder.

Katie returns and crawls next to me, taking my hand away.

She leans over, grabbing my cock, but her attention is on Nick's movement, "You're all in. Oh, god, look at that. Fuck him, baby."

"Suck his cock," Nick grips her head and shoves her down over my dick, forcing her fast and hard as he increases his own pace.

I cover my face, trying to smother my unfiltered moans, trying to hold off the building orgasm, but it's impossible. He pounds into me, and Katie's nearly taking my whole cock in her mouth, "Fuck fuck fuck." I shutter, my entire body clenches up before the avalanche, and my seed spurts into Katie's mouth so hard I'm twitching.

"Oh, fuck," Nick moans just before he swiftly pulls out, yanking his dick at a lightning pace. Katie holds her mouth open, and his body convulses as he cums on her face. He nearly collapses, a hand on the bed to keep him up as he pants, "Holy fuck." He rolls and drops beside me.

Nick and I just breathe, staring up at the ceiling. The intensity of our sex is incapacitating. I hadn't thought it could be like that. It was equal to fucking Katie; that's how much I enjoyed it. I'm afraid to look at Nick. I'm pretty sure during our make-out session, Katie's momentary absence didn't bother us.

He moves first, looking at me, smiling like an idiot, and he holds out his hand. I chuckle, slapping it in a high five. I have no clue what it means, but he's happy, so I'm happy.

"Oh fuck," he gets up with a heavy sigh, slapping my leg. "You enjoy that show?"

Katie's resting against the headboard with her legs on mine, "Immensely. We should have videotaped it."

Nick chuckles and goes to the bathroom. Katie jumps on me, squealing, "He liked it!"

"Yeah, me too."

"Oh my god, that was awesome. Way better than the first time."

Awesome is a good word for it, but also confusing, nerve-wracking, awkward works too.

Nick comes back out and throws himself on his stomach beside me. "I'm exhausted." I rest a hand on his back, near the white scar of his knife wound. I'm on cloud fucking nine.

"I got you that time," he mumbles into his skin.

"You proud of that?" I poke back.

"It was fucking work, of course, I'm proud. I haven't worked out in six weeks. My body's in hell."

"Fatass."

Katie snuggles into my neck, "What a perfect night. I got my two boys back." She reaches over and grabs Nick's hand. He kisses her knuckles.

It is close to perfect.

Close, but not there.

What happened at Dave and Buster's returns, smothering the happiness I feel. On top of it, my secret about my heart is a lingering dark cloud shrouding over me. Both of those topics could easily be erased if I talked about it. It sounds easy, but will it be?

"I got something to say, and I need you both to just be quiet and listen."

It's the only way I'll get through it; I'll bulldoze my way to the truth.

Katie sits, "Are you okay?" She grabs a pillow to cover her naked form.

"Just let me say it."

Nick sits up, pulling the blanket over his lap. "Go for it."

Twenty-Two

Tyler: Letting Go

With Nick and Katie looking at me, I unleash all that I've kept from them. I start with the very beginning of my problems: the attack. I explain how useless I felt. How angry I am. How much blame and guilt I have for letting the guy that stabbed Nick go. I tell them how I searched for him, going to bars. Marco was helping me, found me a guy to get a name and how that man wanted me to relieve him in the bathroom. As I say it out loud, I can't believe I struggled with indecision. I see it so clearly now what that could have done to this relationship.

Katie lays back against the pillow with a hand on her head, "That was a lot."

"I'm not done."

"OH, god."

"At the hospital, they told me I have heart failure. The car accident caused many problems, but I was on medication for a time and in physical therapy that eventually, I was okay. But they always told me I'd have problems in the future as I get older. In plain terms, the scar tissue from the surgery is cutting off circulation to my heart."

"So you'll need surgery again?"

"Not yet. It's got to get way worse."

"It's heart failure; how much worse can it get?"

"A lot. Right now, I'm taking medications, and they're working. They caught it early, so I'm pretty much fine. But as I get older, it will degenerate. Probably in ten years, I'll have surgery. Or even eventually, I'll need a new heart."

"A new heart?"

"I'm young; I'm healthy. I work out. Things I can't do is drink as much. No drugs. I need to eliminate salt from my diet. And no stress."

"No stress? Great, your father's right. We're gonna kill you!" Katie takes off for the bathroom and slams the door.

I lean back. I'm actually happy. I thought she would get way madder about nearly blowing a guy in the bathroom.

"You were told in the hospital." Nick murmurs. "Six weeks ago."

"It's not a big deal. Wasn't that what you said about the AFA?"

Nick gets up, "An eye for an eye doesn't work in a marriage." He pulls on boxers and tosses me a pair before he leans against the dresser with his arms crossed.

I crawl off the bed, but I have to use a towel first to get off all the lube. "We were all going through shit. There was never a good time." I pull on my boxers, approaching.

"So you've already been to the doctor? All those trips to the gym. I knew you were getting fatter."

"Shut up." I quickly look down at my stomach. My abs are perfect. "Liar."

Katie comes out of the bathroom with a new face, smiling like she taped her skin that way. "Okay. So when do you go to the doctor?"

"I've already been."

She glances at Nick with wide eyes and then swings back around and slams the door. I go to the door, knocking gently, "Katie, talk to me, please."

The door whips open, and though her eyes clearly express her rage, she beams, "About what? Time for bed."

"You can still talk to me."

"Apparently, I can't because anything I say will stress you and kill you." She tucks herself in, her back to my side of the bed, and she closes her eyes, pretending to be asleep. I look to Nick for help, but he shakes his head, telling me he's not gonna do a thing. She sits up suddenly, "What was the guy's name?"

I'm surprised to say, "I haven't even looked at it yet. I forgot." Struggling with sucking a stranger's cock threw me out of step.

Katie jumps out of bed and takes off down the stairs. I chase after her, "What are you doing?"

Snowball gets in my way, and I trip, trying to reach Katie as she snatches my pants off the floor. The paper falls out, and I snag it before she can get it. She dives for it. I back up, darting to the other side of the living room.

"Give it to me."

"Why?"

"I'm not letting you go look for trouble. Revenge isn't going to make you feel better."

"It might. Everywhere I look, I'm searching for his face."

Nick sits on the steps, watching, refusing to intervene. But I turn to him to help make her understand, "You know what I'm talking about. Explain it to her."

He blinks at me, silent.

"Have you even thought of the consequences?" She bites, "No, because you're young and stupid. Think about it for a moment. You want to end up in jail or dead? Because I'm pretty sure we're supposed to get married and have a kid. So that doesn't work for me. Let's move on, Tyler."

"How am I supposed to let it go? Huh? I can't forgive, I can't forget. You don't know what it was like to watch him get stabbed. I was helpless just like when my mother died, but I shouldn't have been. I'm grown now. I should have been able to protect him."

"Alright, let's think about it. You find the guy. What do you do? Beat him up? Stab him? Kill him? Any of those, he gets the AFA and we all die."

"So we do nothing?"

"We let the police handle it."

"Yeah, they've done a bang-up job. The two they had are out on bail, and they can't find the guy that almost killed Nick, which I have the name right here. I can do something."

"You know, sometimes I think you love drama and stress because all you do is look for it."

"Rather I be like you? Ignore everything?"

"What? What do I ignore—Know what, never mind. You want to kill yourself for this bullshit? I'm not going to marry you if you're just going to get yourself killed."

"Then don't fucking marry me."

Nick pops up, "Okay, lovebirds, to your corners."

I clench my teeth, watching as she walks to the kitchen, resting her hands on the counter. I run a hand through my hair, sitting on the couch with my elbows on my knees and the name in my hands. I could look at it now and give her the paper and pretend I don't know it. But that would be betrayal, wouldn't it?

Snowball is surprisingly in the kitchen, and Katie curses at her. We are in a middle of a fight, and yet this moment sticks out to me. Snowball never goes to Katie.

"I just want all of this to go away. Would you get out of here!" She yells at the dog. "Following me around for fucking days."

"It's not going to go away," I reply. I snap my fingers, and Snowball jots to my side. I scratch her ears.

"Not with you constantly causing trouble."

"I'm not doing anything," I bite back.

"Guys." Nick interrupts. "Enough already."

Once more, Katie approaches, "Baby, if you don't start letting some of this stuff go, your heart's going to give out. So I don't know if you need some meditation classes or therapy, but you can't keep going like you are."

I get up and toss the paper on the counter. "Do what you want."

She snatches it, and I go outside and sit on the porch. I just gave up the fucking name for what reason? To make her happy? To stop this stupid argument? But how does that help me? How will I ever let this rage inside me get out if I can't put it anywhere?

I'm surprised when Katie comes outside. I don't look at her, keeping my head back against the headrest, staring out at the woods. I should have just kept my mouth shut. I could have had my revenge, and she never had to know.

Katie kneels in front of me and rests her head on my lap.

I don't want to stop being angry. But that's where my problem lies, isn't it? I want to be angry. I want to hold on to the hate.

But why? How does it help me?

She lifts her head, tears dripping down her face. It smothers the fire inside of me, and I feel crazy guilty for ever making her cry. She holds the paper out. "It's your decision." She whimpers. "But I'm asking you to choose me over the name. To choose life over revenge. To let go."

I chew my lip, blinking away tears.

It shouldn't be hard. Katie means everything to me. She is the sun in my world. But I've put so much energy into vengeance these last few weeks that it's become part of who I am. It's grown like a tumor in my gut. I've learned how to balance with the growth. How do I dig it out?

I reach for it, and she lets it slide through her fingers.

I stare at it. The piece of paper represents all the rage I've kept inside. I believed the only way to pop the tumor was to hurt the guy that hurt us. But maybe there is another way to extract it. I can tear it up and throw it out.

I rip it and let the pieces fall from my fingers. I know it's not as easy as that. Maybe I need therapy. But I have to remember that Katie's happiness outweighs my own.

Katie throws herself at me, crying into my shoulder. I squeeze her, thankful for her.

"I'm sorry, Katie."

"Me too."

"I want you for the rest of my life. Help me be better. Teach me to be better." She nods, sniffing, burying her head further into my chest. I nudge her with my nose, "You still want to marry me?"

"Are you gonna die?"

Her pitiful voice makes me chuckle "No, baby. I can live a

long, long time with Heart Failure."

"How long?"

I lie a little, but it's what Nick calls a safe lie where it's for her benefit. "A whole lifetime."

"Then I don't get it."

I smile adoringly at her confusion. "I just need medicine, exercise, and live a boring life. You gonna help me with that?"

She nods enthusiastically, "I can make it super boring."

"Hey," Nick pops out, holding up his phone, "You gave him a thousand dollars?" He accuses, looking at me. "You think money grows on trees?"

Twenty-Three

Tyler: Moving Forward

I was in the dog house for a week, and every day felt like torture. It wasn't that they were ignoring me, which I might have preferred. Instead, each morning there was a new topic about our relationship—cheating, trust, money spending, mental health, physical health, diet. The list went on and on, so when it was time to go, I was ready to leave. Until I had to say goodbye to Katie, that was a kick in the balls.

It's been a month without the two of them. I'm living in a hotel next to the hospital. I'm working 80 to 100 hours a week, and it is mentally and physically exhausted. Even on my day off, I'm on call. I have to answer questions or go in at random times during the day.

I didn't realize how exhausted I would be. How terribly long the days would be. How much my brain is constantly moving.

How lonely life would be.

I'm starting to wonder if this is what I want. I can barely call Nick and Katie. Aside from 2-minute phone calls where I'm half asleep, I've been alone.

It's been a hard transition.

I tried to talk to them about getting a house here and living with me, but they looked at each other like the very idea was frightening, then they promptly changed the subject. They've lived in their town home since they've been married. It's probably hard thinking about leaving. They fought off the HOA. What would be the point in moving? I don't want to push either. They've done enough for me. Can't ask them to buy a house that I can't pay for.

The job is worth the loneliness, though. I've saved someone. Just one so far, but knowing it's possible to save more will keep me coming back.

My main concern is how much can my heart take?

My cardiologist wants me to pick a different career. His suggestions were bird-watching and gardening. Needless to say, they weren't moneymakers. I have to pay back Nick. He has given me everything I want and more. The least I can do is pay him what I owe.

But I'm not going to think of any of that today. It's our three-year anniversary, and I had requested this day off back during the interview process. Nick and Katie are on their way. I've been cleaning the hotel room all morning. I'm typically not a messy person, but I've been beyond the word exhausted and haven't had any energy to do anything but sleep.

A knock on the door, and I'm bounding for it. Katie is breathtaking in a summer sunflower dress with white heels. She glows. I can't believe she managed to get more beautiful.

She squeals, throwing herself on me, and I'm spinning her around, kissing her deeply. I grab her legs, lifting her, and she wraps them around my waist. "I've missed you." I murmur into her skin.

"I've missed you too."

"Happy anniversary." I lay her down on the bed, her dress riding up her hips. My hand spreads on her fat thigh, squeezing. I rotate my hips against her, "I can't wait."

"Me either." Katie pants, forcing me against her.

I unzip my pants and take out my dick. She pushes aside her underwear, and I press my tip against her. She's already wet.

"I've been thinking about you all morning." She admits biting her lip.

I shove in her wetness and stay there. The warmth feels like sinking into a hot tub, dick first. It's the best home, deep and lubricated. She groans into my ear. She pulls her breast out, and my lips are on her nipple. I pound into her over and over again. The bed rattles and squeals.

I listen to her breathing, to her moans, missing everything about her. She cums quickly, and I'm not far behind, stalling all my movements as I release my load inside her. It will be a fucking gallon. I haven't cum in weeks.

I lean up on my elbows and meet her grinning face, "Hi."

"Hi." Katie giggles, kissing me once more.

I ease out, quickly putting a shirt up against her vagina. I dive into the bathroom and use the towel to clean off. She was soaked and got my pants wet with her juices. I throw both items in the full laundry basket before I come back out.

Nick leans against the wall with his arms crossed and a smirk on his face. "You happy?" He asks Katie.

"Very."

I slip up my pants, "Hey, man."

"Hey."

Since he doesn't make the first move, I go and kiss him quickly. "You look good."

"Trimmed my beard."

I rub his face, realizing I've missed him just as much. "Missed a spot."

He dives for the mirror, "Where?"

I sit down next to Katie, "So what are we doing? You want to go around town? Or go hiking somewhere?"

"Nick has a place in mind. Oh crap, my underwear is wet." She shimmies out of it only to squeal as more cum drips down her leg, "Gross!" She runs to the bathroom as Nick and I laugh.

* * *

Though both Nick and I advocate for a panties-free afternoon, Katie makes us stop and get her underwear. Since I got to choose, she has on a black lace throng that is barely wide enough to cover her pussy. Just thinking about it keeps me hard, and I have to maneuver my penis down the side of my leg, so it's not obvious. But with Katie sitting in the backseat with me, I don't know how to stop myself, and I lean in, making out with her.

Nick stops the car, to my surprise. We all step out in front of someone's house. "Who are we visiting?"

"A friend. Come on."

We climb the small hill, Katie holding my hand as we follow the sidewalk to the front steps. It's a big old Victorian house with a big veranda. I've always wanted a house like this. It reminds me of my home in Virginia. My mother used to have flowers all around the outside. It was my chore to water all the plants when I was a kid.

Nick walks right in without knocking, and they both turn to me with broad smiles.

"What's going on?"

"Welcome home."

"What?" A smile is emerging. "You bought a house?"

"We bought a house. It's our house."

"What do you mean?"

"Remember those papers I said they were from my lawyer?"

"For the judge?"

"Well, I lied. They were house papers. You're on the deed."

I grip Nick's shoulder, "That's so illegal. But I'm not even mad, bro. Are you fucking kidding?" I hug him before moving around, diving into the living room, into the kitchen. It's newly renovated with beautiful hardwood floors, white cabinets, marble. No furniture yet. It's open and spacious.

"What about our place in Wilkes Barre?"

"We didn't win the battle against the HOA." He admits. "Plus…" He looks at Katie.

She touches her stomach, "We needed to upgrade."

My eyes widen, "You're pregnant?"

She nods rapidly, and I have her in my arms once more, kissing her over and over. I plop her on her feet and kneel down. I lift her dress, ignoring her weak protests. She's still flat as my hands roam over her abs. "Hi, baby." I murmur as I kiss it, "How far along are you?"

"Twelve weeks."

"No way." That's the farthest she's ever gotten. It's real this time, isn't it? I calculate it real quick, but twelve weeks was right before we were attacked. It could still be Nick's. And though secretly that's a little disappointing, I'm relieved. I don't want to know if it's his or mine. I want it to be ours.

I kiss her belly. When I stand, I grip her ass, lifting her again and her legs wrap around my waist. "You keeping secrets?" I kiss her neck, her breasts, her lips. "I thought secrets were against the law."

"Surprises." She corrects.

"I got a surprise for you." I set her on the counter, letting her pussy feel my hard dick.

"That's not surprising." She laughs, shoving me away.

I go to Nick, kissing him deep, holding him. I feel like I've been deprived, and now all I want is the two of them fucking me together. We are becoming a family, the three of us holding onto each other like an indestructible triangle. It's work, the way we love, but it's so fucking worth it.

Katie squeezes between us, and Nick kisses her, and then I kiss her. "I love you." I murmur against her lips. I kiss Nick, "I love you too."

He weasels out of it, "Ditto. Now let's see the rest of the house."

Twenty-Four

Epilogue

Tyler

You're probably wondering who died, right? I wrote all of this and kept you in suspense. Every page you're waiting for it.

But see, I did you a favor. I prepared you. At least now, when it happens, you'll have a chance at recovery. As you read on, realize I didn't have that warning. I was driving down a sun-soaked highway with no road signs. So when that cliff approached, I didn't even know I was falling until I hit bottom.

When you get there, ask yourself. What would you have done? How would you have reacted? How would you handle it? Because let me tell you, none of your answers fucking matter. You don't know. You can't possibly know.

But there is one thing that remains true.

Time heals. As long as we have it.

Also by M.C. Rivera

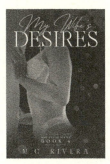

My Wife's Desires Book 4
Are the desires over?

With all of Katie's fantasies finally fulfilled, the polyandry throuple Katie, Nick, and Tyler have finally tied the knot. With a baby on the way, it seems this threesome has really done the impossible. But when tragedy strikes, they must figure out if love is enough to rekindle a dying flame.

This is the concluding novel to MMF Desire Series.

Available Now

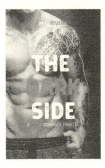

The Dark Side: A Mafia Romance Thriller

Stay up to date with future projects by joining MC Rivera's Newsletter at mcrivera.net